THE WATER-BABIES

by Charles Kingsley
illustrated by Linley Sambourne

being a facsimile edition published by

MAYFLOWER BOOKS
New York
in association with Macmillan

Facsimile Classics Series

ENGLISH FAIRY TALES
by Flora Annie Steel
illustrated by Arthur Rackham

THE WATER-BABIES
by Charles Kingsley
illustrated by Linley Sambourne

THE HEROES OF ASGARD
by A. and E. Keary
illustrated by Charles E. Brock

THE MIKADO
by Sir W. S. Gilbert
illustrated by W. Russell Flint and Charles E. Brock

THE FABLES OF AESOP
edited by Joseph Jacobs
illustrated by Richard Heighway

THE ROMANCE OF KING ARTHUR
by Alfred W. Pollard abridged from Malory
illustrated by Arthur Rackham

THE OTTER STOOD UPRIGHT HALF OUT OF THE WATER, GRINNING
LIKE A CHESHIRE CAT

THE WATER-BABIES

A FAIRY TALE
FOR A LAND-BABY

BY

CHARLES KINGSLEY

ILLUSTRATED BY

LINLEY SAMBOURNE

MACMILLAN AND CO., LIMITED

First published by Macmillan & Co. 1928
First published in this edition 1979 by
MAYFLOWER BOOKS INC.
575 Lexington Avenue New York City 10022

ISBN: 08317-9350-3

Printed in Hong Kong

CONTENTS

CHAPTER I

PAGE

TOM SETS OUT WITH HIS MASTER, MR. GRIMES . . . 1

CHAPTER II

TOM'S EXPERIENCES AT HARTHOVER PLACE . . . 15

CHAPTER III

TOM'S ESCAPE 25

CHAPTER IV

TOM REACHES THE DAME'S SCHOOL 41

CHAPTER V

TOM BECOMES A WATER-BABY 64

CHAPTER VI

TOM'S FIRST EXPERIENCES IN THE WATER 72

CHAPTER VII

TOM MEETS THE OTTER AND THE SALMON—THE STREAM IN
FLOOD 94

CHAPTER VIII

TOM'S ADVENTURES ON HIS WAY TO THE SEA . . . 113

CHAPTER IX

TOM SEES THE LITTLE WHITE LADY AGAIN . . . 129

CONTENTS

CHAPTER X

PAGE

TOM MEETS THE WATER-BABIES 138

CHAPTER XI

THE HOME OF THE WATER-BABIES AND MRS. BEDONEBYAS-
YOUDID 149

CHAPTER XII

TOM'S TEMPTATION AND PUNISHMENT 167

CHAPTER XIII

THE STORY OF THE DOASYOULIKES 187

CHAPTER XIV

TOM'S JOURNEY TO SHINY WALL 200

CHAPTER XV

TOM'S VISIT TO MOTHER CAREY 229

CHAPTER XVI

TOM'S JOURNEY TO THE OTHER-END-OF-NOWHERE, AND HIS
ADVENTURES THEREIN 236

CHAPTER XVII

TOM REACHES MR. GRIMES 258

ILLUSTRATIONS IN COLOUR

Facing page

THE OTTER STOOD UPRIGHT HALF OUT OF THE WATER, GRINNING LIKE A CHESHIRE CAT . . . P. 98 *Frontispiece*

THE MOST BEAUTIFUL LITTLE GIRL THAT TOM HAD EVER SEEN   24

THE CUBS JUMPED OVER HER, AND RAN ROUND HER, AND NIBBLED HER PAWS 33

PLAY BY ME, BATHE IN ME, MOTHER AND CHILD . . . 40

OUT OF ITS BACK ROSE FOUR GREAT WINGS OF BRIGHT BROWN GAUZE 88

ALL THE BOTTOM OF THE STREAM ALIVE WITH GREAT EELS, TURNING AND TWISTING ALONG 105

AT LAST ONE CAME UP BIGGER THAN ALL THE REST . . 112

TOM SAW TWO BRIGHT EYES PEEPING OUT OF THE SAND . 121

TOM HAD NEVER SEEN A LOBSTER BEFORE; AND HE WAS MIGHTILY TAKEN WITH THIS ONE 128

TOM, BETWEEN FRIGHT AND RAGE, TURNED AND BIT THE PROFESSOR'S FINGER TILL IT BLED 137

viii ILLUSTRATIONS IN COLOUR

Facing page

THE LOBSTER SNAPPED OUT OF HIS HAND, AND OUT OF THE
POT, AND SAFE INTO THE SEA 144

TOM BEGGED HER TO TEACH HIM TO BE GOOD AND HELP HIM
TO CURE HIS PRICKLES 176

AN EFT IN A POND 193

THE KING OF THE HERRINGS, WITH A SPRAT IN HIS MOUTH
FOR A CIGAR 208

THAT'S MOTHER CAREY, THERE SHE SITS MAKING OLD BEASTS
INTO NEW ALL THE YEAR ROUND 225

I HAVE BEEN SITTING HERE WAITING FOR YOU MANY A
HUNDRED YEARS 273

CHAPTER I

TOM SETS OUT WITH HIS MASTER, MR. GRIMES

ONCE upon a time there was a little chimney-sweep, and his name was Tom. He lived in a great town in the North country, where there were plenty of chimneys to sweep, and plenty of money for Tom to earn and his master to spend. He could not read nor write, and did not care to do either; and he never washed himself, for there was no water up the

B

court where he lived. He had never been taught to say his prayers. He never had heard of God, or of Christ, except in words which you never have heard, and which it would have been well if he had never heard. He cried half his time, and laughed the other half. He cried when he had to climb the dark flues, rubbing his poor knees and elbows raw; and when the soot got into his eyes, or when his master beat him, or when he had not enough to eat, which happened every day in the week. And he laughed the other half of the day, when he was tossing halfpennies with the other boys, or playing leap-frog over the posts, and thought of the fine times coming, when he would be a man, and a master sweep, and sit in the public-house with a quart of beer and a long pipe, and keep a white bull-dog with one grey ear, and carry her puppies in his pocket, just like a man. And he would have apprentices, one, two,

three, if he could.   How he would bully them,
and knock them about, just as his master did
to him; and make them carry home the soot
bags, while he rode before them on his
donkey, with a pipe in his mouth and a flower

in his button-hole, like a king at the head
of his army.

One day a smart little groom rode into the
court where Tom lived.   Tom was just hiding
behind a wall, to heave half a brick at his
horse's legs, when the groom saw him, and
halloed to him to know where Mr. Grimes,

the chimney-sweep, lived.   Now Mr. Grimes was Tom's own master, so he put the half-brick down quietly behind the wall, and proceeded to take orders.

The groom said that Mr. Grimes was to come up next morning to Sir John Harthover's, at the Place, for the chimneys wanted sweeping.

His master was so delighted at his new customer that he knocked Tom down straight away, and drank more beer that night than he usually did in two.   And when he got up at four the next morning he knocked Tom down again, in order to teach him that he must be an extra good boy that day, as they were going to a very great house, and might make a very good thing of it, if they could but give satisfaction.

And Tom thought so likewise, and would have behaved his best even without being knocked down.

Harthover Place was really a grand place,

even for the rich North country ; with miles
of game-preserves, in which Mr. Grimes and
the collier lads poached at times, and a noble
salmon-river, and Sir John, a grand old man,
whom even Mr. Grimes respected.

So Tom and his master set out ; Grimes
rode the donkey in front, and Tom and the
brushes walked behind ; out of the court, and
up the street, past the closed window-shutters,
and the winking weary policemen, and the
roofs all shining grey in the grey dawn.

They passed through the pitmen's village,

all shut up and silent now; and then they were out in the real country, and plodding along the black dusty road, between black slag walls, with no sound but the groaning and thumping of the pit-engine in the next field. But soon the road grew white, and the walls likewise; and at the wall's foot grew long grass and gay flowers, all drenched with dew; and instead of the groaning of the pit-engine, they heard the skylark saying his matins high up in the air, and the pit-bird warbling in the sedges, as he had warbled all night long.

All else was silent. For old Mrs. Earth was still fast asleep; and, like many pretty people, she looked still prettier asleep than awake. The great elm-trees in the gold-green meadows were fast asleep above, and the cows fast asleep beneath them; nay, the few clouds which were about were fast asleep likewise, and so tired that they had lain down on the earth to rest, in long white flakes and bars, among the stems of the elm-trees, and along the tops of the alders by the stream, waiting for the sun to bid them rise and go about their day's business in the clear blue overhead.

On they went; and Tom looked, and looked, for he never had been so far into the country before; and longed to get over a gate, and pick buttercups, and look for birds' nests in the hedge; but Mr. Grimes was a man of business, and would not have heard of that.

Soon they came up with a poor Irish-woman, trudging along with a bundle at her back. She had a grey shawl over her head, and a crimson petticoat. She had neither shoes nor stockings, and limped along as if she were tired and footsore; but she was a very tall handsome woman, with bright grey eyes, and heavy black hair hanging about her cheeks. And she took Mr. Grimes' fancy so

much, that when he came alongside he called
out to her :

"This is a hard road ; will ye up, lass, and
ride behind me ? "

But, perhaps, she did not like Mr.
Grimes' look and voice ; for she answered
quietly :

"No, thank you : I'd sooner walk with
your little lad here."

"You may please yourself," growled Grimes, and went on smoking.

So she walked beside Tom, and talked to him, and asked him where he lived, and what he knew, and all about himself, till Tom thought he had never met such a pleasant-spoken woman. And she asked him, at last, whether he said his prayers, and seemed sad when he told her that he knew no prayers to say.

Then he asked her where she lived, and she said far away by the sea. And Tom asked her about the sea; and she told him how it rolled and roared over the rocks in winter nights, and lay still in the bright summer days, for the children to bathe and play in it; and many a story more, till Tom longed to go and see the sea, and bathe in it likewise.

At last, at the bottom of a hill, they came to a spring. Out of a low cave of rock, at the foot of a limestone crag, the great fountain rose, and ran away under the road, a stream large enough to turn a mill.

And there Grimes stopped, and looked ; and Tom looked too. Tom was wondering whether anything lived in that dark cave, and came out at night to fly in the meadows. But Grimes was not wondering at all. Without a word, he got off his donkey, and clambered over the low road wall, and knelt down, and began dipping his ugly head into the spring— and very dirty he made it.

Tom was picking the flowers as fast as he could. The Irishwoman helped him, and showed him how to tie them up ; and a very pretty nosegay they had made between them. But when he saw Grimes actually wash, he stopped, quite astonished ; and when Grimes had finished, and began shaking his ears to dry them, he said :

"Why, master, I never saw you do that before."

" Nor will again, most likely. 'Twasn't for cleanliness I did it, but for coolness."

" I wish I might go and dip my head in," said poor little Tom.

" Thou come along," said Grimes; "what dost want with washing thyself? Thou did not drink half a gallon of beer last night, like me."

" I don't care for you," said naughty Tom, and ran down to the stream, and began washing his face.

Grimes was very sulky, because the woman preferred Tom's company to his; so he dashed at him with horrid words, and tore him up from his knees, and began beating him. But Tom was used to that, and got his head safe between Mr. Grimes' legs, and kicked his shins with all his might.

" Are you not ashamed of yourself, Thomas Grimes?" cried the Irishwoman over the wall.

Grimes looked up, startled at her knowing his name; but all he answered was, "No, nor never was yet"; and went on beating Tom.

"True for you. If you ever had been ashamed of yourself, you would have gone over into Vendale long ago."

"What do you know about Vendale?" shouted Grimes; but he left off beating Tom.

"I know about Vendale, and about you, too. I know, for instance, what happened by night two years ago."

"You do?" shouted Grimes; and leaving Tom, he climbed up over the wall, and faced the woman. Tom thought he was going to strike her; but she looked him too full and fierce in the face for that.

"Yes; I was there," said the Irishwoman quietly.

"You are no Irishwoman, by your speech," said Grimes, after many bad words.

"Never mind who I am. I saw what I saw; and if you strike that boy again, I can tell what I know."

Grimes seemed quite cowed, and got on his donkey without another word.

"Stop!" said the Irishwoman. "I have one more word for you both; for you will both see me again before all is over. Those that wish to be clean, clean they will be; and those that wish to be foul, foul they will be. Remember."

And she turned away, and through a gate into the meadow. Grimes stood still a moment, like a man who had been stunned. Then he rushed after her, shouting, "You come back." But when he got into the meadow, the woman was not there.

Had she hidden away? There was no place to hide in. But Grimes looked about, and Tom also, for he was as puzzled as Grimes himself at her disappearing so suddenly ; but look where they would, she was not there.

Grimes came back again, as silent as a post, for he was a little frightened ; and, getting on his donkey, filled a fresh pipe, and smoked away, leaving Tom in peace.

CHAPTER II

AND now they had gone three miles and more, and came to Sir John's lodge-gates.

Very grand lodges they were, with very grand iron gates and stone gate-posts, and on the top of each a most dreadful bogy, all teeth, horns, and tail.

Grimes rang at the gate, and out came a keeper on the spot, and opened.

" I was told to expect thee," he said.

The keeper went with them ; and, to Tom's surprise, he and Grimes chatted together all the way quite pleasantly.

They walked up a great lime avenue, a full mile long, and between their stems Tom peeped trembling at the horns of the sleeping deer, which stood up among the ferns. Tom had never seen such large trees, and as he looked up he fancied that the blue sky rested on their heads. But he was puzzled very

much by a strange murmuring noise, which followed them all the way. So much puzzled, that at last he took courage to ask the keeper what it was.

He spoke very civilly, and called him Sir,

for he was very much afraid of him, which pleased the keeper, and he told him that they were the bees about the lime flowers.

"What are bees?" asked Tom.

"What make honey."

"What is honey?" asked Tom.

"Thou hold thy noise," said Grimes.

"Let the boy be," said the keeper. "He's a civil young chap now, and that's more than he'll be long if he bides with thee."

"I wish I were a keeper," said Tom, "to live in such a beautiful place, and wear green velveteens, and have a real dog-whistle at my button, like you."

The keeper laughed; he was a kind-hearted fellow enough.

By this time they were come up to the great iron gates in front of the house; and Tom stared through them at the rhododendrons and azaleas, which were all in flower; and then at the house itself, and wondered how many

c

chimneys there were in it, and how long ago it
was built, and what was the man's name that
built it, and whether he got much money for his
job?

But Tom and his master did not go in
through the great iron gates, but round the
back way, and a very long way round it was;
and into a little back-door, where the ash-boy
let them in, yawning horribly; and then in a
passage the housekeeper met them, and she
gave Grimes solemn orders about "You will
take care of this, and take care of that," as if he
was going up the chimneys, and not Tom.
And then the housekeeper turned them into a
grand room, all covered up in sheets of brown
paper, and bade them begin; and so after a
whimper or two, and a kick from his master,
into the grate Tom went, and up the chimney,
while a housemaid stayed in the room to watch
the furniture.

How many chimneys Tom swept I cannot

say; but he swept so many that he got quite tired, and puzzled too, for they were not like the town flues to which he was accustomed, but such as you would find in old country-houses, large and crooked chimneys, which had been altered again and again, till they ran one into another. So Tom fairly lost his way in them; but at last, coming down as he thought the right chimney, he came down the wrong one, and found himself standing on the hearthrug in a room the like of which he had never seen before.

Tom had never seen the like. He had never been in gentlefolks' rooms but when the carpets were all up, and the curtains down, and the furniture huddled together under a cloth, and the pictures covered with aprons and dusters; and he had often enough wondered what the rooms were like when they were all ready for the quality to sit in. And now he saw, and he thought the sight very pretty.

The room was all dressed in white,—white window-curtains, white bed-curtains, white furniture, and white walls, with just a few lines of pink here and there. The carpet was all over gay little flowers; and the walls were hung with pictures in gilt frames, which amused Tom very much. There were pictures of ladies and gentlemen, and pictures of horses and dogs. But the two pictures which took his fancy most were, one a man in long garments, with little children and their mothers round him, who was laying his hand upon the children's heads. That was a very pretty picture, Tom thought, to hang in a lady's room. For he could see that it was a lady's room by the dresses which lay about.

The other picture was that of a man nailed to a cross, which surprised Tom much. He fancied that he had seen something like it in a shop-window. But why was it there? "Poor man," thought Tom, "and he looks so kind and quiet. But why should the lady have such a sad picture as that in her room?" And Tom felt sad, and awed, and turned to look at something else.

The next thing he saw, and that too puzzled him, was a washing-stand, with ewers and basins, and soap and brushes, and towels, and a large bath full of clean water—what a heap of things all for washing! "She must be a very dirty lady," thought Tom, thinking of his master, "to want as much scrubbing as all that. But she must be very cunning to put the dirt out of the way so well afterwards, for I don't see a speck about the room, not even on the very towels."

And then, looking toward the bed, he saw that dirty lady, and held his breath with astonishment.

Under the snow-white coverlet, upon the snow-white pillow, lay the most beautiful little girl that Tom had ever seen. Her cheeks were almost as white as the pillow, and her hair was like threads of gold spread all about over the bed.   She might have been as old as Tom, or maybe a year or two older ; but Tom did not think of that. He thought only of her delicate skin and golden hair, and wondered whether she was a real live person, or one of the wax dolls he had seen in the shops. But when he saw her breathe, he made up his mind that she was alive, and stood staring at her, as if she had been an angel out of heaven.

No. She cannot be dirty. She never could have been dirty, thought Tom to himself. And then he thought, "And are all people like that when they are washed?" And he looked at his own wrist, and tried to rub the soot off, and wondered whether it ever would come off. "Certainly I should look much prettier then, if I grew at all like her."

And looking round, he suddenly saw, standing close to him, a little ugly, black, ragged figure, with bleared eyes and grinning white teeth. He turned on it angrily. What did such a little black ape want in that sweet young lady's room? And behold, it was himself, reflected in a great mirror, the like of which Tom had never seen before.

And Tom, for the first time in his life, found out that he was dirty; and burst into tears with shame and anger; and turned to sneak up the chimney again and hide; and upset the fender and threw the fire-irons down, with a noise as of ten thousand tin kettles tied to ten thousand mad dogs' tails.

Up jumped the little white lady in her bed, and, seeing Tom, screamed as shrill as any peacock. In rushed a stout old nurse from the next room, and seeing Tom likewise, made up her mind that he had come to rob, plunder, destroy, and burn; and dashed at him, as he lay over the fender, so fast that she caught him by the jacket.

But she did not hold him.   Tom had been in a policeman's hands many a time, and out of them too, what is more ; and he would have been ashamed to face his friends for ever if he had been stupid enough to be caught by an old woman ; so he doubled under the good lady's arm, across the room, and out of the window in a moment.

THE MOST BEAUTIFUL LITTLE GIRL THAT TOM HAD EVER SEEN

CHAPTER III

TOM'S ESCAPE

HE did not need to drop out, though he would have done so bravely enough. Nor even to let himself down a spout, which would have been an old game to him.

But all under the window spread a tree, with great leaves and sweet white flowers, almost as big as his head. Down the tree he went, like a cat, and across the garden lawn, and over the iron railings, and up the park towards the wood, leaving the old nurse to scream murder and fire at the window.

The under gardener, mowing, saw Tom, and threw down his scythe, and gave chase to poor Tom. The dairymaid heard the noise, got the churn between her knees, and tumbled

over it, spilling all the cream; and yet she
jumped up, and gave chase to Tom. A groom
cleaning Sir John's hack at the stables let him
go loose, ran out, and gave chase to Tom.

Grimes upset the soot-sack in the new-gravelled
yard, and spoilt it all utterly; but he ran out,
and gave chase to Tom. The old steward
opened the park-gate, and gave chase to Tom.
The ploughman left his horses at the headland,
and one jumped over the fence, and pulled the

other into the ditch, plough and all; but he
ran on, and gave chase to Tom. The keeper,
who was taking a stoat out of a trap, let the
stoat go, and caught his own finger; but he

jumped up, and ran after Tom. Sir John
looked out of his study window, ran out, and
gave chase to Tom. The Irishwoman, too,
was walking up to the house to beg; but she
threw away her bundle, and gave chase to Tom
likewise.

In a word, never was there heard such a noise, row, hubbub, babel, shindy, hullabaloo, as that day, when Grimes, gardener, the groom, the dairymaid, Sir John, the steward, the ploughman, the keeper, and the Irish-

woman, all ran up the park, shouting "Stop thief," in the belief that Tom had at least a thousand pounds' worth of jewels in his empty pockets; and the very magpies and jays followed Tom up, screaking and screaming, as if he were a hunted fox.

And all the while poor Tom paddled up the park with his little bare feet, like a small black gorilla fleeing to the forest.

Tom, of course, made for the woods. He had never been in a wood in his life ; but he was sharp enough to know that he might hide in a bush, or swarm up a tree, and, altogether, had more chance there than in the open.

But when he got into the wood, he found it a very different sort of place from what he had fancied. He pushed into a thick cover of rhododendrons, and found himself at once caught in a trap. The boughs laid hold of his legs and arms, poked him in his face and his stomach, made him shut his eyes tight ; and when he got through the rhododendrons, the hassock-grass and sedges tumbled him over, and cut his poor little fingers.

" I must get out of this," thought Tom, " or I shall stay here till somebody comes to help me—which is just what I don't want."

But how to get out was the difficult matter. And indeed I don't think he would ever have got out at all, if he had not suddenly run his head against a wall.

Now running your head against a wall is not pleasant, especially if it is a loose wall, with the stones all set on edge, and a sharp cornered one hits you between the eyes and makes you see all manner of beautiful stars. And so Tom hurt his head ; but he was a brave boy, and did not mind that at all. He guessed that over the wall the cover would end ; and up it he went, and over like a squirrel.

And there he was, out on the great grouse-moors, which the country folk called Harthover Fell—heather and bog and rock, stretching away and up, up to the very sky.

Now, Tom was a cunning little fellow—as cunning as an old Exmoor stag.

He knew as well as a stag that if he backed

he might throw the hounds out. So the first thing he did when he was over the wall was to make the neatest double sharp to his right, and run along under the wall for nearly half a mile.

Whereby Sir John, and the keeper, and the steward, and the gardener, and the ploughman, and the dairymaid, and all the hue-and-cry together, went on ahead half a mile in the very opposite direction, and inside the wall, leaving him a mile off on the outside; while Tom heard their shouts die away in the woods and chuckled to himself merrily.

At last he came to a dip in the land, and went to the bottom of it, and then he turned bravely away from the wall and up the moor; for he knew that he had put a hill between him and his enemies, and could go on without their seeing him.

But the Irishwoman, alone of them all, had seen which way Tom went. She had kept ahead of every one the whole time; and yet she neither walked nor ran. She went along quite smoothly and gracefully, while her feet twinkled past each other so fast that you could not see which was foremost; till every one asked the other who the strange woman was.

When she came to the plantation, they lost sight of her; for she went quietly over the wall after Tom, and followed him wherever he went, and Sir John and the rest saw no more of her.

And now Tom was right away into the heather, but instead of the moor growing flat as he went upwards, it grew more and more broken and hilly, but not so rough but that little Tom could jog along well enough, and find time, too, to stare about at the strange place, which was like a new world to him.

He saw great spiders there, with crowns and crosses marked on their backs, who sat in the middle of their webs, and when they saw Tom coming, shook them so fast that they

THE CUBS JUMPED OVER HER, AND RAN ROUND HER, AND NIBBLED
HER PAWS

became invisible. Then he saw lizards, brown and grey and green, and thought they were snakes, and would sting him; but they were as much frightened as he, and shot away into the heath. And then, under a rock, he saw a pretty sight—a great brown, sharp-nosed creature, with a white tag to her brush, and round her four or five smutty little cubs, the funniest fellows Tom ever saw. She lay on her back, rolling about, and stretching out her legs and head and tail in the bright sunshine; and the cubs jumped over her, and ran round her, and nibbled her paws, and lugged her about by the tail; and she seemed to enjoy it mightily.

And next he had a fright; for, as he scrambled up a sandy brow—whirr-poof-poof-cock-cock-kick—something went off in his face, with a most horrid noise. He thought the ground had blown up, and the end of the world come.

And when he opened his eyes (for he shut them very tight) it was only an old cock-grouse, who had been washing himself in sand, and who, when Tom had all but trodden on him,

jumped up with a noise like the express train, and went off, screaming " Cur-ru-u-uck, cur-ru-u-uck—murder, thieves, fire—cur-u-uck-cock-kick—the end of the world is come—kick-kick-cock-kick."

So Tom went on and on, he hardly knew

why ; but he liked the great wide strange place, and the cool fresh bracing air. But he went more and more slowly as he got higher up the hill ; for now the ground grew very bad indeed. Instead of soft turf and springy heather, he met great patches of flat limestone rock, with deep cracks between the stones and ledges, filled with ferns ; so he had to hop from stone to stone, and now and then he slipped in between, and hurt his little bare toes ; but still he would go on and up, he could not tell why.

What would Tom have said if he had seen, walking over the moor behind him, the very same Irishwoman who had taken his part upon the road ? But whether it was that he looked too little behind him, or whether it was that she kept out of sight behind the rocks and knolls, he never saw her, though she saw him.

And now he began to get a little hungry, and very thirsty ; for he had run a long way, and the sun had risen high in heaven, and the rock was as hot as an oven.

But he could see nothing to eat anywhere, and still less to drink.

The heath was full of bilberries and whimberries; but they were only in flower yet, for it was June. And as for water, who can find that on the top of a limestone rock? Now and then he passed by a deep dark swallow-hole, going down into the earth; and more than once, as he passed, he could hear water falling, trickling, tinkling, many many feet below. How he longed to get down to it, and cool his poor baked lips! But, brave little chimney-sweep as he was, he dared not climb down such chimneys as those.

So he went on and on, till his head spun round with the heat, and he thought he heard church-bells ringing, a long way off.

"Ah!" he thought, "where there is a church there will be houses and people; and, perhaps, some one will give me a bit and a sup." So he set off again, to look for the church; for he was sure that he heard the bells quite plain.

And in a minute more, when he looked round, he stopped again, and said, "Why, what a big place the world is!"

And so it was; for, from the top of the mountain he could see—what could he not see?

Behind him, far below, was Harthover, and the dark woods, and the shining salmon river; and on his left, far below, was the town, and the smoking chimneys of the collieries; and far, far away, the river widened to the shining sea; and little white specks, which were ships, lay on its bosom. Before him lay, spread out like a map, great plains, and farms, and villages, amid dark knots of trees. They all seemed at his very feet; but he had sense to see that they were long miles away.

And to his right rose moor after moor, hill
after hill, till they faded away, blue into blue
sky.   But between him and those moors, and
really at his very feet, lay something, to which,
as soon as Tom saw it, he determined to go,
for that was the place for him.

A deep, deep green and rocky valley, very
narrow, and filled with trees; but through the
wood, hundreds of feet below him, he could see
a clear stream glance.   Oh, if he could but get
down to that stream!   Then, by the stream, he
saw the roof of a little cottage, and a little
garden set out in squares and beds.   And
there was a tiny little red thing moving
in the garden, no bigger than a fly.   As Tom
looked down, he saw that it was a woman in a
red petticoat.   Ah! perhaps she would give
him something to eat.   And there were the
church-bells ringing   again. Surely   there
must be a village down there.   Well, nobody
would know him, or what had happened at

the Place. The news could not have got there yet, even if Sir John had set all the policemen in the county after him; and he could get down there in five minutes.

Tom was quite right about the hue-and-cry not having got thither; for he had come, without knowing it, the best part of ten miles from Harthover; but he was wrong about getting down in five minutes, for the cottage was more than a mile off, and a good thousand feet below.

However, down he went, like a brave little man as he was, though he was very footsore, and tired, and hungry, and thirsty; while the church-bells rang so loud, he began to think that they must be inside his own head, and the river chimed and tinkled far below; and this was the song which it sang:—

Clear and cool, clear and cool,
By laughing shallow, and dreaming pool ;
Cool and clear, cool and clear,
By shining shingle, and foaming wear ;

Under the crag where the ouzel sings,
And the ivied wall where the church-bell rings,
Undefiled, for the undefiled ;
Play by me, bathe in me, mother and child.

Dank and foul, dank and foul,
By the smoky town in its murky cowl ;
Foul and dank, foul and dank,
By wharf and sewer and slimy bank ;
Darker and darker the farther I go,
Baser and baser the richer I grow ;
Who dare sport with the sin-defiled ?
Shrink from me, turn from me, mother and child.

Strong and free, strong and free,
The floodgates are open, away to the sea,
Free and strong, free and strong,
Cleansing my streams as I hurry along,
To the golden sands, and the leaping bar,
And the taintless tide that awaits me afar.
As I lose myself in the infinite main,
Like a soul that has sinned and is pardoned again.
Undefiled, for the undefiled ;
Play by me, bathe in me, mother and child.

So Tom went down; and all the while he
never saw the Irishwoman going down behind
him.

PLAY BY ME, BATHE IN ME, MOTHER AND CHILD

CHAPTER IV

TOM REACHES THE DAME'S SCHOOL

A MILE off, and a thousand feet down.

So Tom found it; though it seemed as if he could have thrown a pebble on to the back of the woman in the red petticoat who was weeding in the garden, or even across the dale to the rocks beyond. For the bottom of the valley was just one field broad, and on the other side ran the stream; and above it, grey crag, grey down, grey stair, grey moor walled up to heaven.

So Tom went to go down; and first he went down three hundred feet of steep heather, mixed up with loose brown gritstone, as rough as a file; which was not pleasant to his poor little heels, as he came bump, stump, jump, down the steep. And still he thought he could throw a stone into the garden.

Then he went down three hundred feet of limestone terraces, one below the other, as straight as if a carpenter had ruled them with his ruler and then cut them out with his chisel. There was no heath there, but—

First, a little grass slope, covered with the prettiest flowers, rockrose and saxifrage, and thyme and basil, and all sorts of sweet herbs.

Then bump down a two-foot step of limestone.

Then another bit of grass and flowers.

Then bump down a one-foot step.

Then another bit of grass and flowers for fifty yards, as steep as the house roof, where he had to slide down.

Then another step of stone, ten feet high ; and there he had to stop himself, and crawl along the edge to find a crack ; for if he had rolled over, he would have rolled right into the old woman's garden, and frightened her out of her wits.

Then, when he had found a dark narrow crack, full of fern, and had crawled down through it, with knees and elbows, as he would down a chimney, there was another grass slope, and another step, and so on, till—oh, dear me! I wish it was all over; and so did he. And yet he thought he could throw a stone into the old woman's garden.

At last he came to a bank of beautiful shrubs; whitebeam with its great silver-backed leaves, and mountain-ash, and oak; and below them cliff and crag, cliff and crag, with great beds of crown-ferns and wood-sedge; while through the shrubs he could see the stream sparkling, and hear it murmur on the white pebbles. He did not know that it was three hundred feet below.

You would have been giddy, perhaps, at looking down : but Tom was not. He was a brave little chimney-sweep; and when he found himself on the top of a high cliff, instead of sitting down and crying, he said, " Ah, this will just suit me!" though he was very tired ; and down he went, by stock and stone, sedge and ledge, bush and rush, as if he had been born a jolly little black ape, with four hands instead of two.

And all the while he never saw the Irish-woman coming down behind him.

But he was getting terribly tired now. The burning sun on the fells had sucked him up; but the damp heat of the woody crag sucked him up still more; and the perspiration ran out of the ends of his fingers and toes, and washed him cleaner than he had been for a whole year. But, of course, he dirtied every-thing terribly as he went. There has been a great black smudge all down the crag ever since.

At last he got to the bottom. But behold,

it was not the bottom—as people usually find
when they are coming down a mountain. For
at the foot of the crag were heaps and heaps
of fallen limestone, with holes between them
full of sweet heath-fern ; and before Tom got
through them, he was out in the bright sunshine again ; and then he felt, once for all and
suddenly, as people generally do, that he was
b-e-a-t, beat.

He could not get on. The sun was burning,
and yet he felt chill all over. He was quite
empty, and yet he felt quite sick. There was
but two hundred yards of smooth pasture
between him and the cottage, and yet he could
not walk down it. He could hear the stream
murmuring only one field beyond it, and yet it
seemed to him as if it was a hundred miles
off.

He lay down on the grass till the beetles
ran over him, and the flies settled on his nose.
I don't know when he would have got up

again, if the gnats and the midges had not taken compassion on him. But the gnats blew their trumpets so loud in his ear, and the midges nibbled so at his hands and face wherever they could find a place free from soot, that at last he woke up, and stumbled away, down over a low wall, and into a narrow road, and up to the cottage-door.

And a neat pretty cottage it was, with clipped yew hedges all round the garden.

He came slowly up to the open door, which was all hung round with clematis and roses; and then peeped in, half afraid.

And there sat by the empty fireplace the nicest old woman that ever was seen, in her red petticoat, and short dimity bedgown, and clean white cap, with a black silk handkerchief over it, tied under her chin. At her feet sat the grandfather of all the cats; and opposite her sat, on two benches, twelve or fourteen neat, rosy, chubby little children, learning

their letters ; and gabble enough they made
about it.

All the children started at Tom's dirty
black figure,—the girls began to cry, and the
boys began to laugh, and all pointed at him
rudely enough ; but Tom was too tired to care
for that.

"What art thou, and what dost want?"
cried the old · dame. "A chimney-sweep!
Away with thee ! I'll have no sweeps here."

" Water," said poor little Tom, quite faint.

"Water? There's plenty i' the beck," she
said, quite sharply.

" But I can't get there ; I'm most clemmed
with hunger and drought." And Tom sank
down upon the door-step, and laid his head
against the post.

And the old dame looked at him through
her spectacles one minute, and two, and three ;
and then she said, " He's sick ; and a bairn's
a bairn, sweep or none."

"Water," said Tom.

"God forgive me!" and she put by her spectacles, and rose, and came to Tom. "Water's bad for thee; I'll give thee milk." And she toddled off into the next room, and brought a cup of milk and a bit of bread.

Tom drank the milk off at one draught, and then looked up, revived.

"Where didst come from?" said the dame.

"Over Fell, there," said Tom, and pointed up into the sky.

"Over Harthover? and down Lewthwaite Crag? Art sure thou are not lying?"

"Why should I?" said Tom, and leant his head against the post.

"And how got ye up there?"

"I came over from the Place"; and Tom was so tired and desperate he had no heart or time to think of a story, so he told all the truth in a few words.

'Bless thy little heart! And thou hast not been stealing, then?"

" No."

"Bless thy little heart! and I'll warrant not. Why, God's guided the bairn, because he was innocent! Away from the Place, and over Harthover Fell, and down Lewthwaite Crag! Who ever heard the like, if God hadn't led him? Why dost not eat thy bread?"

" I can't."

"It's good enough, for I made it myself."

" I can't," said Tom, and he laid his head on his knees, and then asked—

" Is it Sunday?"

" No, then ; why should it be?"

" Because I hear the church-bells ringing so."

" Bless thy pretty heart! The bairn's sick. Come wi' me, and I'll hap thee up somewhere. If thou wert a bit cleaner I'd put thee in my own bed, for the Lord's sake. But come along here."

E

But when Tom tried to get up, he was so tired and giddy that she had to help him and lead him.

She put him in an outhouse upon soft sweet hay and an old rug, and bade him sleep off his walk, and she would come to him when school was over, in an hour's time.

And so she went in again, expecting Tom to fall fast asleep at once.

But Tom did not fall asleep.

Instead of it he turned and tossed and kicked about in the strangest way, and felt so hot all over that he longed to get into the river and cool himself; and then he fell half asleep, and dreamt that he heard the little white lady crying to him, "Oh, you're so dirty; go and be washed"; and then that he heard the Irish-woman saying, "Those that wish to be clean, clean they will be." And then he heard the church-bells ring so loud, close to him too, that he was sure it must be Sunday, in spite of what the old dame had said ; and he would go to church, and see what a church was like inside, for he had never been in one, poor little fellow, in all his life. But the people would never let him come in, all over soot and dirt like that. He must go to the river and wash first. And he said out loud again and again, though being half asleep he did not know it, " I must be clean, I must be clean."

And all of a sudden he found himself, not in the outhouse on the hay, but in the middle of a meadow, over the road, with the stream just before him, saying continually, " I must be clean, I must be clean." He had got there on his own legs, between sleep and awake, as children will often get out of bed, and go about the room, when they are not quite well. But he was not a bit surprised, and went on to the bank of the brook, and lay down on the grass, and looked into the clear, clear limestone water, with every pebble at the bottom bright and clean, while the little silver trout dashed about in fright at the sight of his black face; and he dipped his hand in and found it so cool, cool, cool; and he said, "I will be a fish; I will swim in the water; I must be clean, I must be clean."

So he pulled off all his clothes in such haste that he tore some of them, which was easy enough with such ragged old things. And he put his poor hot sore feet into the water; and then his legs; and the farther he went in, the more the church-bells rang in his head.

"Ah," said Tom, "I must be quick and wash myself; the bells are ringing quite loud now; and they will stop soon, and then the door will be shut, and I shall never be able to get in at all."

And all the while he never saw the Irish-woman, not behind him this time, but before.

For just before he came to the river side, she had stept down into the cool clear water;

and her shawl and her petticoat floated off her, and the green water-weeds floated round her sides, and the white water-lilies floated round her head, and the fairies of the stream came up from the bottom and bore her away and down upon their arms; for she was the Queen of them all; and perhaps of more besides.

"Where have you been?" they asked her.

"I have been smoothing sick folks' pillows, and whispering sweet dreams into their ears; opening cottage casements, to let out the stifling air; coaxing little children away from gutters, and foul pools where fever breeds; turning women from the gin-shop door, and staying men's hands as they were going to strike their wives; doing all I can to help those who will not help themselves: and little enough that is, and weary work for me. But I have brought you a new little brother, and watched him safe all the way here."

Then all the fairies laughed for joy at the thought that they had a little brother coming.

"But mind, maidens, he must not see you, or know that you are here. He is but a savage now, and like the beasts which perish; and from the beasts which perish he must learn. So you must not play with him, or speak to him, or let him see you: but only keep him from being harmed."

Then the fairies were sad, because they could not play with their new brother, but they always did what they were told.

And their Queen floated away down the river; and whither she went, thither she came. But all this Tom, of course, never saw or heard; for he was so hot and thirsty, and longed so to be clean for once, that he tumbled himself as quick as he could into the clear cool stream.

And he had not been in it two minutes before he fell fast asleep, into the quietest, sunniest, cosiest sleep that ever he had in his life; and he dreamt about the green meadows by which he had walked that morning, and the tall elm-trees, and the sleeping cows; and after that he dreamt of nothing at all.

The reason of his falling into such a delightful sleep is very simple; and yet hardly any one has found it out. It was merely that the fairies took him.

Some people think that there are no fairies, but we will make believe that there are fairies in the world. There must be fairies; for this is a fairy tale: and how can one have a fairy tale if there are no fairies?

The kind old dame came back at twelve, when school was over, to look at Tom: but there was no Tom there. She looked about for his footprints; but the ground was so hard that there was not one to be seen anywhere.

So the old dame went in again quite sulky, thinking that little Tom had tricked her with a false story, and shammed ill, and then run away again.

But she altered her mind the next day. For, when Sir John and the rest of them had run themselves out of breath, and lost Tom, they went back again, looking very foolish.

And they looked more foolish still when Sir John heard more of the story from the nurse; and more foolish still, again, when they heard the whole story from Miss Ellie, the little lady in white. All she had seen was a poor little black chimney-sweep, crying and sobbing, and going to get up the chimney again. Of course, she was very much frightened : and no wonder. But that was all. The boy had taken nothing in the room; by the mark of his little sooty feet, they could see that he had never been off the hearthrug till the nurse caught hold of him. It was all a mistake.

So Sir John told Grimes to go home, and promised him five shillings if he would bring the boy quietly up to him, without beating him, that he might be sure of the truth. For he took for granted, and Grimes too, that Tom had made his way home.

But no Tom came back to Mr. Grimes that evening; and he went to the police-office, to tell them to look out for the boy. But no Tom was heard of. As for his having gone over those great fells to Vendale, they no more dreamed of that than of his having gone to the moon.

So Mr. Grimes came up to Harthover next day with a very sour face; but when he got there, Sir John was over the hills and far away; and Mr. Grimes had to sit in the outer servants' hall all day, and wait until Sir John came back.

For good Sir John had slept very badly that night; and he said to his lady, " My dear, the boy must have got over into the grouse-moors, and lost himself."

So, at five the next morning up he got, and into his bath, and into his shooting-jacket and gaiters, and into the stable-yard, and bade them

bring his shooting pony, and the keeper to come on his pony, and the huntsman, and the first whip, and the second whip, and the under-keeper with the bloodhound in a leash —a great dog as tall as a calf, of the colour of a gravel-walk, with mahogany ears and nose, and a throat like a church-bell. They took him up to the place where Tom had gone into the wood; and there the hound lifted up his mighty voice, and told them all he knew.

Then he took them to the place where Tom had climbed the wall; and they shoved it down, and all got through.

And then the wise dog took them over the moor, and over the fells, step by step, very slowly; for the scent was a day old, you know, and very light from the heat and drought. But that was why cunning old Sir John started at five in the morning.

And at last he came to the top of Lewthwaite Crag, and there he bayed, and looked up in their faces, as much as to say, " I tell you he is gone down here!"

They could hardly believe that Tom would have gone so far; and when they looked at that awful cliff, they could never believe that he would have dared to face it. But if the dog said so, it must be true.

"Heaven forgive us!" said Sir John. "If we find him at all, we shall find him lying at the bottom." And he slapped his great hand upon his great thigh, and said—

"Who will go down over Lewthwaite Crag, and see if that boy is alive? Oh that I were twenty years younger, and I would go down myself!" And so he would have done, as well as any sweep in the county. Then he said—

"Twenty pounds to the man who brings me that boy alive!" and, as was his way, what he said he meant.

Now among the lot was a little groom-boy, a very little groom indeed; and he was the same who had ridden up the court, and told Tom to come to the Hall; and he said—

"Twenty pounds or none, I will go down

over Lewthwaite Crag, if it's only for the poor boy's sake. For he was as civil a spoken little chap as ever climbed a flue."

So down over Lewthwaite Crag he went : a very smart groom he was at the top, and a very shabby one at the bottom ; for he tore his gaiters, and he tore his breeches, and he tore his jacket, and he burst his braces, and he burst his boots, and he lost his hat, and what was worst of all, he lost his shirt pin, which he prized very much, for it was gold : but he never saw anything of Tom.

And all the while Sir John and the rest were riding round, full three miles to the right, and back again, to get into Vendale, and to the foot of the crag.

When they came to the old dame's school, all the children came out to see. And the old dame came out too ; and when she saw Sir John, she curtsied very low, for she was a tenant of his.

"Well, dame, and how are you?" said Sir John.

"Blessings on you as broad as your back, Harthover," says she—she didn't call him Sir John, but only Harthover, for that is the fashion in the North country—"and welcome into Vendale: but you're no hunting the fox this time of the year?"

"I am hunting, and strange game too," said he.

"Blessings on your heart, and what makes you look so sad the morn?"

"I'm looking for a lost child, a chimney-sweep, that is run away."

"Oh, Harthover, Harthover," says she, "ye'll no harm the poor little lad if I give you tidings of him?"

"Not I, not I, dame. I'm afraid we hunted him out of the house all on a miserable mistake, and the hound has brought him to the top of Lewthwaite Crag, and——"

Whereat the old dame broke out crying, without letting him finish his story.

"So he told me the truth after all, poor little dear!" And then she told Sir John all.

"Bring the dog here, and lay him on," said Sir John, without another word, and he set his teeth very hard.

And the dog opened at once; and went away at the back of the cottage, over the road, and over the meadow, and through a bit of alder copse; and there, upon an alder stump, they saw Tom's clothes lying. And then they knew as much about it all as there was any need to know.

CHAPTER V

TOM BECOMES A WATER-BABY

AND Tom?

Ah, now comes the most wonderful part of this wonderful story. Tom, when he woke, for of course he woke—children always wake after they have slept exactly as long as is good for them—found himself swimming about in the stream, being about four inches long, and having round his neck a set of gills just like those of a sucking eft, which he mistook for a lace frill, till he pulled at them, found he hurt himself, and made up his mind that they were part of himself, and best left alone.

In fact, the fairies had turned him into a water-baby.

A water-baby? You never heard of a water-baby. Perhaps not. That is the very reason why this story was written. There are a great many things in the world which you never

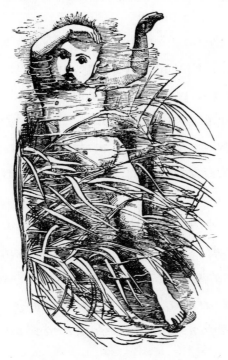

heard of; and a great many more which nobody ever heard of.

"But there are no such things as water-babies."

F

How do you know that? Have you been there to see? And if you had been there to see, and had seen none, that would not prove that there were none.

No water-babies, indeed? Why, wise men of old said that everything on earth had its double in the water. There are land-babies— then why not water-babies? *Are there not water-rats, water-flies, water-crickets, water-crabs, water-tortoises, water-scorpions, water-tigers and water-hogs, water-cats and water-dogs, sea-lions and sea-bears, sea-horses and sea-elephants, sea-mice and sea-urchins, sea-razors and sea-pens, sea-combs and sea-fans; and of plants, are there not water-grass, and water-crowfoot, water-milfoil, and so on, without end?*

"But all these things are only nicknames; the water things are not really akin to the land things."

That's not always true. They are, in

millions of cases, not only of the same family, but actually the same individual creatures. Do not even you know that a green drake, and an alder-fly, and a dragon-fly, live under water till they change their skins, just as Tom changed his? And if a water animal can continually change into a land animal, why should not a land animal sometimes change into a water animal?

But at all events, so it happened to Tom. And, therefore, the keeper, and the groom, and Sir John made a great mistake, and were very unhappy (Sir John at least) without any reason, when they found a black thing in the water, and said it was Tom's body, and that he had been drowned. They were utterly mistaken. Tom was quite alive; and cleaner, and merrier, than he ever had been. The fairies had washed him, you see, in the swift river, so thoroughly, that not only his dirt, but his whole husk and shell had been washed quite off him, and the pretty little real Tom was washed out of the inside of it, and swam away, as a caddis does when its case of stones and silk is bored through, and away it goes on its back, paddling to the shore, there to split its skin, and fly away as a caperer, on four fawn-coloured wings, with long legs and horns. They are foolish fellows, the caperers, and fly into the candle at night, if you leave the door open. We will hope Tom will be wiser, now he has got safe out of his sooty old shell.

But good Sir John did not understand all this, and he took it into his head that Tom was drowned. When they looked into the empty pockets of his shell, and found no jewels there, nor money—nothing but three marbles, and a brass button with a string to it—then Sir John did something as like crying as ever he did in his life, and blamed himself more bitterly than he need have done. So he cried, and the groom-boy cried, and the huntsman cried, and the dame cried, and the little girl cried, and the dairymaid cried, and the old nurse cried (for it was somewhat her fault), and my lady cried; but the keeper did not cry, though he had been so good-natured to Tom the morning before; for he was so dried up with running after poachers, that you could no more get tears out of him than milk out of leather: and Grimes did not cry, for Sir John gave him ten pounds, and he drank it all in a week. And the little girl would not play with her dolls for a whole week, and never forgot poor little Tom. And soon my lady put a pretty little tombstone over Tom's shell in the little churchyard in Vendale, where the old dalesmen all sleep side by side between the limestone crags. And the dame decked it with garlands every Sunday, till she grew so old that she could not stir abroad; then the little children decked it for her. And always she sang an old old song, as she sat spinning what she called her wedding-dress.

The children could not understand it, but they liked it none the less for that; for it was very sweet, and very sad; and that was enough for them. And these are the words of it :—

When all the world is young, lad,
And all the trees are green ;
And every goose a swan, lad,
And every lass a queen ;
Then hey for boot and horse, lad,
And round the world away ;
Young blood must have its course, lad,
And every dog his day.

When all the world is old, lad,
And all the trees are brown ;
And all the sport is stale, lad,
And all the wheels run down ;
Creep home, and take your place there,
The spent and maimed among ;
God grant you find one face there,
You loved when all was young.

Those are the words : but they are only the body of it : the soul of the song was the dear old woman's sweet face, and sweet voice, and the sweet old air to which she sang ; and that, alas! one cannot put on paper. And at last

she grew so stiff and lame, that the angels were
forced to carry her; and they helped her on
with her wedding-dress, and carried her up
over Harthover Fells, and a long way beyond

that too; and there was a new schoolmistress
in Vendale.

And all the while Tom was swimming
about in the river, with a pretty little lace-
collar of gills about his neck, as lively as a
grig, and as clean as a fresh-run salmon.

CHAPTER VI

TOM'S FIRST EXPERIENCES IN THE WATER

TOM was now quite amphibious, which means that he was both an animal and a fish : and what is better still, he was clean. For the first time in his life, he felt how comfortable it was to have nothing on him but himself. But he only enjoyed it : he did not know it, or think about it; just as you enjoy life and health, and yet never think about being alive and healthy.

He did not remember having ever been dirty. Indeed, he did not remember any of his old troubles, being tired, or hungry, or beaten, or sent up dark chimneys. Since that sweet sleep, he had forgotten all about his master, and Harthover Place, and the little white girl, and in a word, all that had happened to him when he lived before; and what was best of all, he had forgotten all the bad words which he had learned from Grimes, and the rude boys with whom he used to play.

That is not strange: for you know, when you came into this world, and became a land-baby, you remembered nothing. So why should he, when he became a water-baby?

But Tom was very happy in the water. He had been sadly overworked in the land-world; and so now, to make up for that, he had nothing but holidays in the water-world for a long, long time to come. He had nothing to do now but enjoy himself, and look at all the pretty things which are to be seen in the cool clear water-world, where the sun is never too hot, and the frost is never too cold.

And what did he live on? Water-cresses, perhaps; or perhaps water-gruel, and water-milk.

Sometimes he went along the smooth gravel
water-ways, looking at the crickets which ran
in and out among the stones, as rabbits do on
land; or he climbed over the ledges of rock,

and saw the sand-pipes hanging in thousands,
with every one of them a pretty little head and
legs peeping out; or he went into a still corner,
and watched the caddises eating dead sticks as
greedily as you would eat plum-pudding, and
building their houses with silk and glue. Very
fanciful ladies they were; none of them would

keep to the same materials for a day. One
would begin with some pebbles ; then she would
stick on a piece of green wood ; then she found
a shell, and stuck it on too ; and the poor shell
was alive, and did not like at all being taken
to build houses with ; then she stuck on a
piece of rotten wood, then a very smart pink
stone, and so on, till she was patched all over
like an Irishman's coat. Then she found a
long straw, five times as long as herself, and
said, "Hurrah! my sister has a tail, and I'll
have one too"; and she stuck it on her back,
and marched about with it quite proud, though
it was very inconvenient indeed. And, at that,
tails became all the fashion among the caddis-
baits in that pool, and they all toddled about
with long straws sticking out behind, getting
between each other's legs, and tumbling over
each other, and looking so ridiculous, that Tom
laughed at them till he cried.

Then sometimes he came to a deep still

reach; and there he saw the water-forests. They would have looked to you only little weeds: but Tom, you must remember, was so little that everything looked a hundred times as big to him as it does to you, just as things do to a minnow, who sees and catches the little water-creatures which you can only see in a microscope.

And in the water-forest he saw the water-monkeys and water-squirrels (they had all six legs, though; everything almost has six legs in the water, except efts and water-babies); and nimbly enough they ran among the branches. There were water-flowers there too, in thousands; and Tom tried to pick them: but as soon as he touched them, they drew themselves in and turned into knots of jelly; and then Tom saw that they were all alive—bells, and stars, and wheels, and flowers, of all beautiful shapes and colours; and all alive and busy, just as Tom was. So now he found that there

was a great deal more in the world than he had
fancied at first sight.

There was one wonderful little fellow, too,

who peeped out of the top of a house built of
round bricks. He had two big wheels, and one
little one, all over teeth, spinning round and
round like the wheels in a thrashing-machine;
and Tom stood and stared at him, to see what

he was going to make with his machinery. And what do you think he was doing? Brick-making. With his two big wheels he swept together all the mud which floated in the water : all that was nice in it he put into his stomach and ate; and all the mud he put into the little wheel on his breast, which really was a round hole set with teeth ; and there he spun it into a neat hard round brick ; and then he took it and stuck it on the top of his house-wall, and set to work to make another. Now was not he a clever little fellow?

Tom thought so: but when he wanted to talk to him the brick-maker was much too busy and proud of his work to take notice of him.

Now you must know that all the things under the water talk; only not such a language as ours; but such as horses, and dogs, and cows, and birds talk to each other; and Tom soon learned to understand them and talk to them; so that he might have had very pleasant company if he had only been a good boy. But I am sorry to say, he was too like some other little boys, very fond of hunting and tormenting creatures for mere sport. Some people say that boys cannot help it; that it is nature. But whether it is nature or not, little boys can help it, and must help it. For if they have naughty, low, mischievous tricks in their nature, as monkeys have, that is no reason why they should give way to those tricks like monkeys, who know no better. And therefore they must not torment dumb creatures; for if they do, a certain old lady who is coming will surely give them exactly what they deserve.

But Tom did not know that; and he pecked and howked the poor water-things about sadly, till they were all afraid of him, and got out of his way, or crept into their shells; so he had no one to speak to or play with.

The water-fairies, of course, were very sorry

to see him so unhappy, and longed to take him, and tell him how naughty he was, and teach him to be good, and to play and romp with him too: but they had been forbidden to do that. Tom had to learn his lesson for himself by sound and sharp experience.

At last one day he found a caddis, and wanted it to peep out of its house: but its house-door was shut. He had never seen a caddis with a house-door before: so what must he do, the meddlesome little fellow, but pull it open, to see what the poor lady was doing inside. What a shame! How should you like to have any one breaking your bed-room-door in, to see how you looked when you were in bed? So Tom broke to pieces the door, which was the prettiest little grating of silk, stuck all over with shining bits of crystal; and when he looked in, the caddis poked out her head, and it had turned into just the shape of a bird's. But when Tom spoke to her she could not answer; for her mouth and face were tight tied up in a new night-cap of neat pink skin. However, if she didn't answer, all the other caddises did; for they held up their hands and shrieked like the cats in Struwwelpeter: "*Oh, you nasty horrid boy; there you are at it again! And she had just laid herself up for a fortnight's sleep, and then she would have come out with such beautiful wings, and flown about, and laid such lots of eggs: and now you have broken her door, and she can't mend it because her mouth is tied up for a fortnight, and she will die. Who sent you here to worry us out of our lives?*"

So Tom swam away. He was very much ashamed of himself, and felt all the naughtier; as little boys do when they have done wrong and won't say so.

Then he came to a pool full of little trout, and began tormenting them, and trying to catch them: but they slipped through his fingers, and jumped clean out of water in their fright. But as Tom chased them, he came close to a great dark hole under an alder root, and out floushed a huge old brown trout ten

times as big as he was, and ran right against him, and knocked all the breath out of his body; and I don't know which was the more frightened of the two.

Then he went on sulky and lonely, as he deserved to be; and under a bank he saw a

very ugly dirty creature sitting, about half as
big as himself; which had six legs, and a big
stomach, and a most ridiculous head with two
great eyes and a face just like a donkey's.

"Oh," said Tom, "you are an ugly fellow
to be sure!" and he began making faces at
him; and put his nose close to him, and
halloed at him, like a very rude boy.

When, hey presto; all the thing's donkey-
face came off in a moment, and out popped a
long arm with a pair of pincers at the end of
it, and caught Tom by the nose. It did not
hurt him much; but it held him quite tight.

"Yah, ah! Oh, let me go!" cried Tom.

"Then let me go," said the creature. "I
want to be quiet. I want to split."

Tom promised to let him alone, and he let
go. "Why do you want to split?" said Tom.

"Because my brothers and sisters have
all split, and turned into beautiful creatures
with wings; and I want to split too. Don't

speak to me. I am sure I shall split. I will split!"

Tom stood still, and watched him. And he swelled himself, and puffed, and stretched himself out stiff, and at last—crack, puff, bang—he opened all down his back, and then up to the top of his head.

And out of his inside came the most slender, elegant, soft creature, as soft and smooth as Tom: but very pale and weak, like a little child who has been ill a long time in a dark room. It moved its legs very feebly; and looked about it half ashamed; and then it began walking slowly up a grass stem to the top of the water.

Tom was so astonished that he never said a word: but he stared with all his eyes. And he went up to the top of the water too, and peeped out to see what would happen.

And as the creature sat in the warm bright sun, a wonderful change came over it. It grew strong and firm ; the most lovely colours began to show on its body, blue and yellow and black, spots and bars and rings ; out of its back rose four great wings of bright brown gauze ; and its eyes grew so large that they filled all its head, and shone like ten thousand diamonds.

"Oh, you beautiful creature ! " said Tom ; and he put out his hand to catch it.

But the thing whirred up into the air, and hung poised on its wings a moment, and then settled down again by Tom quite fearless.

" No ! " it said, " you cannot catch me. I am a dragon-fly now, the king of all the flies ; and I shall dance in the sunshine, and hawk over the river, and catch gnats, and have a beautiful wife like myself. I know what I shall do. Hurrah ! " And he flew away into the air, and began catching gnats.

"Oh ! come back, come back," cried Tom, "you beautiful creature. I have no one to play with, and I am so lonely here. If you will but come back I will never try to catch you."

"I don't care whether you do or not," said the dragon-fly; "for you can't. But when I have had my dinner, and looked a little about this pretty place, I will come back, and have a little chat about all I have seen in my travels. Why, what a huge tree this is! and what huge leaves on it!"

It was only a big dock: but you know the dragon-fly had never seen any but little water-trees; so it did look very big to him.

The dragon-fly did come back, and chatted away with Tom. He was a little conceited about his fine colours and his large wings; but you know, he had been a poor dirty ugly creature all his life before; so there were great excuses for him. He was very fond of talking about all the wonderful things he saw in the trees and the meadows; and Tom liked to listen to him, for he had forgotten all about them. So in a little while they became great friends.

And I am very glad to say, that Tom learned such a lesson that day, that he did not torment creatures for a long time after. And then the caddises grew quite tame, and used to tell him strange stories about the way they built their houses, and changed their skins, and turned at last into winged flies; till Tom began to long to change his skin, and have wings like them some day.

And the trout and he made it up (for trout very soon forget if they have been frightened and hurt). So Tom used to play with them at hare and hounds, and great fun they had; and he used to try to leap out of the water, head over heels, as they did before a shower came on; but somehow he never could manage it. He liked most, though, to see them rising at the flies, as they sailed round and round under the shadow of the great oak, where the beetles fell flop into the water, and the green caterpillars let themselves down from the boughs by silk ropes for no reason at all ; and then changed their foolish minds for no reason at all either ; and hauled themselves up again into the tree, rolling up the rope in a ball between their paws.

And very often Tom caught them just as they touched the water ; and caught the alder-flies, and the caperers, and the cock-tailed duns and spinners, yellow, and brown, and claret, and grey, and gave them to his friends the trout. Perhaps he was not quite kind to the flies ; but one must do a good turn to one's friends when one can.

And at last he gave up catching even the flies ; for he made acquaintance with one by accident and found him a very merry little fellow. And this was the way it happened ; and it is all quite true.

OUT OF ITS BACK ROSE FOUR GREAT WINGS OF BRIGHT BROWN GAUZE

He was basking at the top of the water one hot day in July, catching duns and feeding the trout, when he saw a new sort, a dark grey little fellow with a brown head.. He was a very little fellow indeed : but he made the most of himself, as people ought to do. He cocked up his head, and he cocked up his wings, and he cocked up his tail, and he cocked up the two whisks at his tail-end, and, in short, he looked the cockiest little man of all little men. And so he proved to be ; for instead of getting away, he hopped upon Tom's finger, and he cried out in the tiniest, shrillest, squeakiest little voice you ever heard,

"Much obliged to you, indeed ; but I don't want it yet."

"Want what?" said Tom, quite taken aback by his impudence.

"Your leg, which you are kind enough to hold out for me to sit on. I must just go and see after my wife for a few minutes. Dear

me! what a troublesome business a family
is!" (though the idle little rogue did nothing
at all, but left his poor wife to lay all the eggs
by herself). "When I come back, I shall be
glad of it, if you'll be so good as to keep it
sticking out just so"; and off he flew.

Tom thought him a very cool sort of per-
sonage; and still more so, when, in five minutes
he came back, and said—"Ah, you were tired
waiting? Well, your other leg will do as well."

And he popped himself down on Tom's
knee, and began chatting away in his squeaking
voice.

"So you live under the water? It's a low
place. I lived there for some time; and was
very shabby and dirty. But I didn't choose
that that should last. So I turned respectable,
and came up to the top, and put on this grey
suit. It's a very business-like suit, you think,
don't you?"

"Very neat and quiet indeed," said Tom.

"Yes, one must be quiet and neat and respectable, and all that sort of thing for a little, when one becomes a family man. But I'm tired of it, that's the truth. I've done quite enough business, I consider, in the last week, to last me my life. So I shall put on a ball dress, and go out and be a smart man, and see the gay world, and have a dance or two. Why shouldn't one be jolly if one can?"

"And what will become of your wife?"

"Oh! she is a very plain, stupid creature, and that's the truth ; and thinks about nothing but eggs. If she chooses to come, why she may; and if not, why I go without her ;—and here I go."

And as he spoke he turned quite pale, and then quite white.

"Why, you're ill!" said Tom. But he did not answer.

"You're dead," said Tom, looking at him as he stood on his knee as white as a ghost.

"No, I ain't!" answered a little squeaking voice over his head. "This is me up here, in my ball-dress; and that's my skin. Ha, ha! you could not do such a trick as that!"

And no more Tom could, nor all the conjurors in the world. For the little rogue had jumped clean out of his own skin, and left it standing on Tom's knee, eyes, wings, legs, tail, exactly as if it had been alive.

"Ha, ha!" he said, and he jerked and skipped up and down, never stopping an instant, just as if he had St. Vitus's dance. "Ain't I a pretty fellow now?"

And so he was; for his body was white, and his tail orange, and his eyes all the colours of a peacock's tail. And, what was the oddest of all, the whisks at the end of his tail had grown five times as long as they were before.

"Ah!" said he, "now I will see the gay world. My living won't cost me much, for I have no mouth, you see, and no inside; so I can never be hungry nor have the stomach-ache neither."

No more he had. He had grown as dry and hard and empty as a quill, as such silly shallow-hearted fellows deserve to grow.

But, instead of being ashamed of his emptiness, he was quite proud of it, as a good many fine gentlemen are, and began flirting and flipping up and down, and singing—

" My wife shall dance, and I shall sing,
So merrily pass the day ;
For I hold it quite the wisest thing,
To drive dull care away."

And he danced up and down for three days and three nights, till he grew so tired, that he tumbled into the water, and floated down. But what became of him Tom never knew, and he himself never minded ; for Tom heard him singing to the last, as he floated down—

" To drive dull care away-ay-ay ! "

And if he did not care, why nobody else cared either.

CHAPTER VII

TOM MEETS THE OTTER AND THE SALMON
THE STREAM IN FLOOD

BUT one day Tom had a new adventure. He was sitting on a water-lily leaf, he and his friend the dragon-fly, watching the gnats dance. The dragon-fly had eaten as many as he wanted, and was sitting quite still and sleepy, for it was very hot and bright, and kept on chatting to Tom about the times when he lived under the water.

Suddenly, Tom heard the strangest noise up the stream; cooing, and grunting, and whining, and squeaking.

He looked up the water, and there he saw a sight as strange as the noise; a great ball rolling over and over down the stream, seeming one moment of soft brown fur, and the next

of shining glass: and yet it was not a ball;
for sometimes it broke up and streamed away
in pieces, and then it joined again; and all
the while the noise came out of it louder and
louder.

Tom asked the dragon-fly what it could be:
but, with his short sight, he could not even see
it, though it was not ten yards away. So he
took the neatest little header into the water,
and started off to see for himself; and, when
he came near, the ball turned out to be four or
five beautiful creatures, many times larger
than Tom, who were swimming about, and
rolling, and diving, and twisting, and wrest-
ling, and cuddling, and kissing, and biting,
and scratching, in the most charming fashion
that ever was seen.

But, when the biggest of them saw Tom,
she darted out from the rest, and cried, "Quick,
children, here is something to eat, indeed!"
and came at poor Tom, showing such a wicked

pair of eyes, and such a set of sharp teeth in
a grinning mouth, that Tom slipped in between
the water-lily roots as fast as he could, and then
turned round and made faces at her.

"Come out," said the wicked old otter, "or
it will be worse for you."

But Tom looked at her from between two
thick roots, and shook them with all his might,
making horrible faces all the while, just as he
used to grin through the railings at the old
women, when he lived before.

"Come away, children," said the otter in disgust, "it is not worth eating, after all. It is only a nasty eft, which nothing eats."

"I am not an eft!" said Tom; "efts have tails."

"You are an eft," said the otter, very positively; "I see your two hands quite plain, and I know you have a tail."

"I tell you I have not," said Tom. "Look here!" and he turned his pretty little self quite round; and sure enough, he had no more tail than you.

"I say you are an eft, and therefore you are, and not fit food for me and my children. You may stay there till the salmon eat you (she knew the salmon would not, but she wanted to frighten poor Tom). Ha! ha! they will eat you, and we will eat them"; and the otter laughed such a wicked cruel laugh.

"What are salmon?" asked Tom.

"Fish, you eft, great fish, nice fish to eat.

H

We hunt them up and down the pools, and drive them up into a corner, the silly things ; and we catch them, but we disdain to eat them all ; we just bite out their soft throats and suck their sweet juice—Oh, so good !"—(and she licked her wicked lips)—"and then throw them away, and go and catch another. They are coming soon, children, coming soon ; I can smell the rain coming up off the sea, and then hurrah for salmon, and plenty of eating all day long."

And the otter grew so proud that she turned head over heels twice, and then stood upright half out of the water, grinning like a Cheshire cat.

"And where do they come from ?" asked Tom, who kept himself very close, for he was very frightened.

"Out of the sea, eft, the great wide sea, where they might stay and be safe if they liked. But out of the sea the silly things come, into the great river down below, and we come up to watch for them ; and when they go down again we go down and follow them. And there we fish for the bass and the pollock, and have jolly days along the shore, and toss and roll in the breakers, and sleep snug in the warm dry crags. Ah, that is a merry life too, children, if it were not for those horrid men."

"What are men?" asked Tom ; but somehow he seemed to know before he asked.

"Two-legged things, eft : and, now I come to look at you, they are actually something like you, if you had not a tail, only a great deal bigger ; and they catch the fish with hooks and lines, which get into our feet sometimes, and set pots along the rocks to catch lobsters. They speared my poor dear husband as he went out to find something for me to eat, and I saw them carrying him away upon a pole."

And the otter grew so sad that she sailed solemnly away down the burn, and Tom saw

her no more for that time. And lucky it was
for her that she did so ; for no sooner was she
gone, than down the bank came seven little
rough terrier dogs, snuffing and yapping, and
grubbing and splashing, in full cry after the
otter. Tom hid among the water-lilies till
they were gone; for he could not guess that
they were the water-fairies come to help
him.

But he could not help thinking of what the
otter had said about the great river and the
broad sea. And, as he thought, he longed to
go and see them. He could not tell why ; but
the more he thought, the more he grew discontented with the narrow little stream in
which he lived, and all his companions there ;
and wanted to get out into the wide wide
world, and enjoy all the wonderful sights.

And once he set off to go down the stream.
But the stream was very low ; and when he
came to the shallows he could not keep under

water, for there was no water left to keep
under. So the sun burned his back and made
him sick; and he went back again and lay
quiet in the pool for a whole week more.

And then, on the evening of a very hot day,
he saw a sight.

He had been very stupid all day, and so
had the trout; for they would not move an
inch to take a fly, though there were thousands
on the water, but lay dozing at the bottom
under the shade of the stones; and Tom lay
dozing too, for the water was quite warm and
unpleasant.

But toward evening it grew suddenly dark,
and Tom looked up and saw a blanket of black
clouds lying right across the valley above his
head. He felt not quite frightened, but very
still; for everything was still. There was not
a whisper of wind, nor a chirp of a bird to be
heard; and next a few great drops of rain fell
plop into the water, and one hit Tom on the

nose, and made him pop his head down quickly enough.

And then the thunder roared, and the lightning flashed, and leapt across Vendale and back again, from cloud to cloud, and cliff to cliff, till the very rocks in the stream seemed to shake : and Tom looked up at it through the water, and thought it the finest thing he ever saw in his life.

But out of the water he dared not put his head ; for the rain came down by bucketsful ; and soon the stream rose, and rushed down, higher and higher, and fouler and fouler, full of beetles, and sticks, and straws, and worms, and addle-eggs, and wood-lice, and leeches, and other creatures that live in pools.

Tom could hardly stand against the stream, and hid behind a rock. But the trout did not ; for out they rushed from among the stones, and began gobbling the beetles and leeches in the most greedy and quarrelsome way, and swimming about with great worms hanging out of their mouths, tugging and kicking to get them away from each other.

And now, by the flashes of the lightning, Tom saw a new sight—all the bottom of the stream alive with great eels, turning and twisting along, all down stream and away. They had been hiding for weeks past in the cracks of the rocks, and in burrows in the mud; and Tom had hardly ever seen them, except now and then at night: but now they were all out, and went hurrying past him so fiercely and wildly that he was quite frightened. And as they hurried past he could hear them say to each other, "We must run, we must run. What a jolly thunderstorm! Down to the sea, down to the sea!"

And then the otter came by with all her brood, twining and sweeping along as fast as the eels themselves; and she spied Tom as she came by, and said:

"Now is your time, eft, if you want to see the world. Come along, children, never mind those nasty eels : we shall breakfast on salmon to-morrow. Down to the sea, down to the sea !"

Then came a flash brighter than all the rest, and by the light of it—in the thousandth part of a second they were gone again—but he had seen them, he was certain of it—Three beautiful little white girls, with their arms twined round each other's necks, floating down the torrent, as they sang, "Down to the sea, down to the sea !"

"Oh stay! Wait for me !" cried Tom ; but they were gone : yet he could hear their voices clear and sweet through the roar of thunder and water and wind, singing as they died away, "Down to the sea !"

"Down to the sea ?" said Tom ; "everything is going to the sea, and I will go too. Good-bye, trout."

ALL THE BOTTOM OF THE STREAM ALIVE WITH GREAT EELS, TURNING
AND TWISTING ALONG

And now, down the rushing stream, guided by the bright flashes of the storm; past tall rocks; on through narrow strids and roaring cataracts, where Tom was deafened and blinded for a moment by the rushing waters; along deep reaches, where the white water-lilies tossed and flapped beneath the wind and hail; past sleeping villages; under dark bridge-arches, and away and away to the sea. And Tom could not stop, and did not care to stop; he would see the great world below, and the salmon, and the breakers, and the wide wide sea.

And when the daylight came, Tom found himself out in the salmon river.

Tom thought nothing about what the river was like. All his fancy was, to get down to the wide wide sea.

And after a while he came to a place where the river spread out into broad still shallow reaches, so wide that little Tom, as he put his head out of the water, could hardly see across.

And there he stopped. He got a little frightened. "This must be the sea," he thought. "What a wide place it is! If I go on into it I shall surely lose my way, or some strange thing will bite me. I will stop here and look out for the otter, or the eels, or some one to tell me where I shall go."

So he went back a little way, and crept into a crack of the rock, just where the river opened out into the wide shallows, and watched for some one to tell him his way: but the otter and the eels were gone on miles and miles down the stream.

There he waited, and slept too, for he was quite tired with his night's journey; and, when he woke, the stream was clearing to a beautiful amber hue, though it was still very high. And after a while he saw a sight which made him jump up; for he knew in a moment it was one of the things which he had come to look for.

Such a fish ! ten times as big as the biggest trout, and a hundred times as big as Tom, sculling up the stream past him, as easily as Tom had sculled down.

Such a fish ! shining silver from head to tail, and here and there a crimson dot ; with a grand hooked nose and grand curling lip, and a grand bright eye, looking round him as proudly as a king. Surely he must be the salmon, the king of all the fish.

Tom was so frightened that he longed to creep into a hole ; but he need not have been ; for salmon are all true gentlemen, and they never harm or quarrel with any one, but go about their own business, and leave rude fellows to themselves.

The salmon looked at him full in the face, and then went on without minding him, with a swish or two of his tail which made the stream boil again. And in a few minutes came another, and then four or five, and so on ; and all passed Tom, rushing and plunging up the cataract with strong strokes of their silver tails, now and then leaping clean out of water and up over a rock, shining gloriously for a moment in the bright sun ; while Tom was so delighted that he could have watched them all day long.

And at last one came up bigger than all the rest ; but he came slowly, and stopped, and looked back, and seemed very anxious and busy, and Tom saw that he was helping another salmon.

"My dear," said the great fish to his companion, "you really look dreadfully tired, and you must not over-exert yourself at first. Do rest yourself behind this rock " ; and he shoved her gently with his nose, to the rock where Tom sat, for this was the salmon's wife.

Then he saw Tom, and looked at him very

fiercely one moment, as if he was going to bite
him.

"What do you want here?" he said, very
fiercely.

"Oh, don't hurt me!" cried Tom. "I
only want to look at you; you are so handsome."

"Ah?" said the salmon, very stately but
very civilly. "I really beg your pardon; I see
what you are, my little dear. I have met one
or two creatures like you before, and found
them very agreeable and well-behaved. Indeed, one of them showed me a great kindness
lately, which I hope to be able to repay. I
hope we shall not be in your way here. As
soon as this lady is rested, we shall proceed
on our journey."

What a well-bred old salmon he was!

"So you have seen things like me before?"
asked Tom.

"Several times, my dear. Indeed, it was

only last night that one at the river's mouth came and warned me and my wife of some new stake-nets which had got into the stream, I cannot tell how, since last winter, and showed us the way round them, in the most charmingly obliging way."

"So there are babies in the sea?" cried Tom, and clapped his little hands. "Then I shall have some one to play with there? How delightful!"

"Were there no babies up this stream?" asked the lady salmon.

"No! and I grew so lonely. I thought I saw three last night; but they were gone in an instant, down to the sea. So I went too; for I had nothing to play with but caddises and dragon-flies and trout."

"Poor little dear!" said the lady; "but how sad for him to live among such people as caddises, who have actually six legs, the nasty things; and dragon-flies, too! why, they are not even good to eat; for I tried them once, and they are all hard and empty; and, as for trout, every one knows what they are."

"Why do you dislike the trout so?" asked Tom.

"My dear, we do not even mention them, if we can help it; for I am sorry to say they are relations of ours who do us no credit. A great many years ago they were just like us: but they were so lazy, and cowardly, and greedy, that instead of going down to the sea every year to see the world and grow strong and fat, they chose to stay and poke about in the little streams and eat worms and grubs; and they are very properly punished for it; for they have grown ugly and brown and spotted and small; and actually will eat our children."

So the salmon went up, after Tom had warned them of the wicked old otter; and Tom went down, but slowly and cautiously, coasting along the shore.

AT LAST ONE CAME UP BIGGER THAN ALL THE REST

CHAPTER VIII

HE was many days about it, for it was many miles down to the sea; and perhaps he would never have found his way, if the fairies had not guided him, without his seeing their fair faces, or feeling their gentle hands.

And, as he went, he had a very strange adventure. It was a clear still September night, and the moon shone so brightly down through the water, that he could not sleep, though he shut his eyes as tight as possible. So at last he came up to the top, and sat upon a little point of rock, and looked up at the broad yellow moon, and wondered what she was, and thought that she looked at him. And he watched the moonlight on the rippling river,

and the black heads of the firs ; and listened
to the owl's hoot, and the fox's bark, and
the otter's laugh ; and smelt the soft perfume
of the wafts of heather honey off the grouse-
moor far above ; and felt very happy, though
he could not tell why. You, of course, would
have been very cold sitting there on a September night, without the least bit of clothes on
your wet back ; but Tom was a water-baby,
and therefore felt cold no more than a fish.

Suddenly, he saw a beautiful sight. A
bright red light moved along the river-side,
and threw down into the water a long taproot
of flame. Tom, curious little rogue that he
was, must needs go and see what it was ; so he
swam to the shore, and met the light as it
stopped over a shallow run at the edge of a
low rock.

And there, underneath the light, lay five
or six great salmon, looking up at the flame
with their great goggle eyes, and wagging

their tails, as if they were very much pleased at it.

Tom came to the top, to look at this wonderful light nearer, and made a splash.

And he heard a voice say :

" There was a fish rose."

He did not know what the words meant : but he seemed to know the sound of them, and to know the voice which spoke them ; and he saw on the bank three great two-legged creatures, one of whom held the light, flaring and sputtering, and another a long pole. And he knew that they were men, and was frightened, and crept into a hole in the rock, from which he could see what went on.

The man with the torch bent down over the water, and looked earnestly in ; and then he said :

" Tak' that muckle fellow, lad ; he's ower fifteen punds ; and haud your hand steady."

Tom felt that there was some danger

coming, and longed to warn the foolish salmon, who kept staring up at the light as if he was bewitched. But before he could make up his mind, down came the pole through the water; there was a fearful splash and struggle, and Tom saw that the poor salmon was speared right through, and was lifted out of the water.

And then, from behind, there sprang on these three men three other men; and there were shouts, and blows, and words which Tom recollected to have heard before; and he shuddered and turned sick at them now, for he felt somehow that they were strange, and ugly, and wrong, and horrible. And it all began to come back to him. They were men; and they were fighting; savage, desperate, up-and-down fighting, such as Tom had seen too many times before.

And he stopped his little ears, and longed to swim away; and was very glad that he was a

water-baby, and had nothing to do any more
with horrid dirty men, with foul clothes on
their backs, and foul words on their lips; but
he dared not stir out of his hole: while the
rock shook over his head with the trampling
and struggling of the keepers and the poachers.

All of a sudden there was a tremendous
splash, and a frightful flash, and a hissing, and
all was still.

For into the water, close to Tom, fell one
of the men; he who held the light in his hand.
Into the swift river he sank, and rolled over
and over in the current. Tom heard the men
above run along, seemingly looking for him;
but he drifted down into the deep hole below,
and there lay quite still, and they could not
find him.

Tom waited a long time, till all was quiet;
and then he peeped out, and saw the man
lying. At last he screwed up his courage and
swam down to him "Perhaps," he thought,

"the water has made him fall asleep, as it did me."

Then he went nearer. He grew more and more curious, he could not tell why. He must go and look at him. He would go very quietly, of course; so he swam round and round him, closer and closer; and, as he did not stir, at last he came quite close and looked him in the face.

The moon shone so bright that Tom could see every feature; and, as he saw, he recollected, bit by bit, it was his old master, Grimes.

Tom turned tail, and swam away as fast as he could.

"Oh dear me!" he thought, "now he will turn into a water-baby. What a nasty troublesome one he will be! And perhaps he will find me out, and beat me again."

So he went up the river again a little way, and lay there the rest of the night under an alder root ; but, when morning came, he longed to go down again to the big pool, and see whether Mr. Grimes had turned into a water-baby yet.

So he went very carefully, peeping round all the rocks, and hiding under all the roots. Mr. Grimes lay there still ; he had not turned into a water-baby. In the afternoon Tom went back again. He could not rest till he had found out what had become of Mr. Grimes. But this time Mr. Grimes was gone ; and Tom made up his mind that he was turned into a water-baby.

He might have made himself easy, poor little man ; Mr. Grimes did not turn into a water-baby, or anything like one at all. He could not know that the fairies had carried him away, and put him, where they put everything which falls into the water, exactly where it ought to be.

Then Tom went on down, for he was afraid

of staying near Grimes: and as he went, all
the vale looked sad. The red and yellow
leaves showered down into the river; the flies
and beetles were all dead and gone; the chill
autumn fog lay low upon the hills, and sometimes spread itself so thickly on the river that
he could not see his way.   But he felt his way
instead, following the flow of the stream, day
after day, past great bridges, past boats and
barges, past the great town, with its wharfs,
and mills, and tall smoking chimneys, and
ships which rode at anchor in the stream; and
now and then he ran against their hawsers,
and wondered what they were, and peeped out,
and saw the sailors lounging on board smoking
their pipes; and ducked under again, for he
was terribly afraid of being caught by man and
turned into a chimney-sweep once more. He
did not know that the fairies were close to him
always, shutting the sailors' eyes lest they
should see him, and turning him aside from all

TOM SAW **TWO** BRIGHT EYES PEEPING OUT OF THE SAND

foul and dangerous things. Poor little fellow, it was a dreary journey for him; and more than once he longed to be back in Vendale, playing with the trout in the bright summer sun. But it could not be. What has been once can never come over again. And people can be little babies, even water-babies, only once in their lives.

But Tom was always a brave, determined little English boy, who never knew when he was beaten; and on and on he held, till he saw a long way off the red buoy through the fog. And then he found, to his surprise, the stream turned round, and running up inland.

It was the tide, of course: but Tom knew nothing of the tide. He only knew that in a minute more the water, which had been fresh, turned salt all round him. And then there came a change over him. He felt strong, and light, and fresh; and gave, he did not know

why, three skips out of the water, a yard high,
and head over heels, just as the salmon do
when they first touch the noble rich salt
water.

He did not care now for the tide being
against him. The red buoy was in sight,
dancing in the open sea; and to the buoy he
went. He passed great shoals of bass and
mullet, leaping and rushing in after the shrimps,
but he never heeded them, or they him; and

once he passed a great black shining seal, who
was coming in after the mullet. The seal put
his head and shoulders out of water, and stared
at him. And Tom, instead of being frightened,
said, " How d'ye do, sir ; what a beautiful place

the sea is !" And the old seal, instead of
trying to bite him, looked at him with his soft
sleepy winking eyes, and said, " Good tide to
you, my little man ; are you looking for your
brothers and sisters ? I passed them all at
play outside."

"Oh, then," said Tom, " I shall have playfellows at last," and he swam on to the buoy, and got upon it (for he was quite out of breath) and sat there, and looked round for water-babies : but there were none to be seen.

The sea-breeze came in freshly with the tide and blew the fog away; and the little waves danced for joy around the buoy, and the old buoy danced with them. The gulls laughed like girls at play, and the sea-pies, with their red bills and legs, flew to and fro from shore to shore, and whistled sweet and wild. And Tom looked and looked, and listened; and he would have been very happy, if he could only have seen the water-babies. Then when the tide turned, he left the buoy, and swam round and round in search of them : but in vain. Sometimes he thought he heard them laughing : but it was only the laughter of the ripples. And sometimes he thought he saw them at the bottom : but it was only white and pink shells. And once he was sure he had found one, for he saw two bright eyes peeping out of the sand. So he dived down, and began scraping the sand away, and cried, "Don't hide; I do want some one to play with so much!" And out jumped a great turbot with his ugly eyes and mouth all awry, and flopped away along the bottom, knocking poor Tom over. And he sat down at the bottom of the sea, and cried salt tears from sheer disappointment.

Tom sat upon the buoy long days, long weeks, looking out to sea, and wondering when the water-babies would come back; and yet they never came.

Then he began to ask all the strange things which came in out of the sea if they had seen any; and some said "Yes," and some said nothing at all.

He asked the bass and the pollock; but they were so greedy after the shrimps that they did not care to answer him a word.

And then there came by a beautiful creature, like a ribbon of pure silver with a sharp head and very long teeth; but it seemed very sick and sad. Sometimes it rolled helpless on its side; and then it dashed away glittering like white fire; and then it lay sick again and motionless.

"Where do you come from?" asked Tom. "And why are *you* so sick and sad?"

"I come from the warm Carolinas, but I wandered north and north, till I met with the cold icebergs, afloat in the mid ocean. So I got tangled amongst the icebergs, and chilled with their frozen breath. But the water-babies helped me from among them, and set me free again. And now I am mending every day; but I am very sick and sad; and perhaps I shall never get home again."

"Oh!" cried Tom. "And you have seen water-babies? Have you seen any near here?"

"Yes; they helped me again last night, or

I should have been eaten by a great black porpoise."

How vexatious! The water-babies close to him, and yet he could not find one.

And then he left the buoy, and used to go along the sands and round the rocks, and come out in the night and sit upon a point of rock, among the shining seaweeds, in the low October tides, and cry and call for the water-babies; but he never heard a voice call in return. And at last, with his fretting and crying, he grew quite lean and thin.

But one day among the rocks he found a playfellow. It was not a water-baby, alas! but it was a lobster.

Tom had never seen a lobster before; and he was mightily taken with this one; for he thought him the most curious, odd, ridiculous creature he had ever seen.

He had one claw knobbed and the other jagged; and Tom delighted in watching him hold on to the seaweed with his knobbed claw, while he cut up salads with his jagged one, and then put them into his mouth, after smelling at them, like a monkey.

Tom asked him about water-babies. "Yes," he said. He had seen them often. But he did not think much of them. They were meddlesome little creatures, that went about helping fish and shells which got into scrapes. Well, for his part, he should be ashamed to be helped by little soft creatures that had not even a shell on their backs. He had lived quite long enough in the world to take care of himself.

He was a conceited fellow, the old lobster, and not very civil to Tom. But he was so funny, and Tom so lonely, that he could not quarrel with him; and they used to sit in holes in the rocks, and chat for hours.

TOM HAD NEVER SEEN A LOBSTER BEFORE; AND HE WAS MIGHTILY
TAKEN WITH THIS ONE

CHAPTER IX

TOM SEES THE LITTLE WHITE LADY AGAIN

AND about this time there happened to Tom a very strange and important adventure—so important, indeed, that he was very near never finding the water-babies at all; and I am sure you would have been sorry for that.

I hope that you have not forgotten the little white lady all this while. At least, here she comes, looking like a clean white good little darling, as she always was, and always will be. For it befell in the pleasant short December days, that Sir John was so busy hunting that nobody at home could get a word out of him. Whereon My Lady determined to go off and leave him, so she started for the seaside with all the children.

But where she went to nobody must know, for fear young ladies should begin to fancy that there are water-babies there!

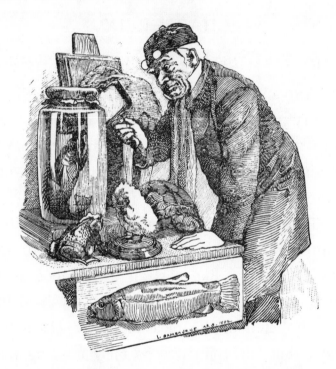

Now it befell that, on the very shore, and over the very rocks, where Tom was sitting with his friend the lobster, there walked one day the little white lady, Ellie herself, and

with her a very wise man indeed—Professor
Ptthmllnsprts.

He was a very worthy kind good-natured
little old gentleman; and very fond of children.
He had met Sir John somewhere or other, and

had made acquaintance with him, and become very fond of his children.

Ellie and he were walking on the rocks, and he was showing her about one in ten thousand of all the beautiful and curious things which are to be seen there. But little Ellie was not satisfied with them at all. She liked much better to play with live children, or even with dolls, which she could pretend were alive; and at last she said, "I don't care about all these things, because they can't play with me, or talk to me. If there were little children now in the water, as there used to be, and I could see them, I should like that."

"Children in the water, you strange little girl?" said the professor.

"Yes," said Ellie. "I know there used to be children in the water, and mermaids too, and mermen. I saw them all in a picture at home, of a beautiful lady sailing in a car drawn by dolphins, and babies flying round her, and one sitting in her lap; and the mermaids swimming and playing, and the mermen trumpeting on conch-shells; and it is called "The Triumph of Galatea"; and there is a burning mountain in the picture behind. It hangs on the great staircase, and I have looked at it ever since I was a baby, and dreamt about it a hundred times; and it is so beautiful, that it must be true." But the professor would not agree to this, and said that no man was forced to believe anything to be true, but what he could see, hear, taste, or handle.

Now little Ellie was, I suppose, a stupid little girl; for, instead of being convinced by Professor Ptthmllnsprts' arguments, she only asked the same question over again.

"But why are there not water-babies?"

I trust and hope that it was because the professor trod at that moment on the edge of a very sharp mussel, and hurt one of his corns sadly, that he answered quite sharply:

" Because there ain't."

Which was not even good English, for the professor ought to have said, if he was so angry as to say anything of the kind—Because there are not: or are none: or are none of them ; or because they do not exist.

And he groped with his net under the weeds so violently, that he caught poor little Tom.

He felt the net very heavy ; and lifted it out quickly, with Tom all entangled in the meshes.

" Dear me ! " he cried.

And he took him out.

" It has actually eyes ! " he cried.   " This is most extraordinary ! "

" It is a water-baby ! " cried Ellie ; and of course it was.

" Water-fiddlesticks, my dear ! " said the professor ; and he turned away sharply.

There was no denying it.   It was a water-baby : and he had said a moment ago that there were none.   What was he to do ?

He would have liked, of course, to have taken Tom home in a bucket. But what would Ellie say, after what he had just told her? He hesitated a moment. He longed to keep Tom, and yet he half wished he never had caught him; and at last he quite longed to get rid of him. So he turned away and poked Tom with his finger, for want of anything better to do; and said carelessly, "My dear little maid, you must have dreamt of water-babies last night, your head is so full of them."

Now Tom had been in the most horrible fright all the while; and had kept as quiet as he could; for it was fixed in his little head that if a man with clothes on caught him, he might put clothes on him too, and make a dirty black chimney-sweep of him again. But, when the professor poked him, it was more than he could bear; and, between fright and rage, he turned and bit the professor's finger till it bled.

"Oh! ah! yah!" cried he; and glad of an

excuse to be rid of Tom, dropped him on to the seaweed, and thence he dived into the water and was gone in a moment.

"But it was a water-baby, and I heard it speak!" cried Ellie. "Ah, it is gone!" And she jumped down off the rock to try and catch Tom before he slipped into the sea.

Too late! and what was worse, as she sprang down, she slipped, and fell some six feet, with her head on a sharp rock, and lay quite still.

The professor picked her up, and tried to waken her, and called to her, and cried over her, for he loved her very much : but she would not waken at all. So he took her up in his arms and carried her to her governess, and they all went home; and little Ellie was put to bed, and lay there quite still; only now and then she woke up and called out about the water-baby : but no one knew what she meant, and the professor did not tell, for he was ashamed to tell.

TOM, BETWEEN FRIGHT AND RAGE, TURNED AND BIT THE PROFESSOR'S
FINGER TILL IT BLED

And, after a week, one moonlight night, the fairies came flying in at the window and brought her such a pretty pair of wings that she could not help putting them on ; and she flew with them out of the window, and over the land, and over the sea, and up through the clouds, and nobody heard or saw anything of her for a very long while.

And this is why they say that no one has ever yet seen a water-baby.

CHAPTER X

TOM MEETS THE WATER-BABIES

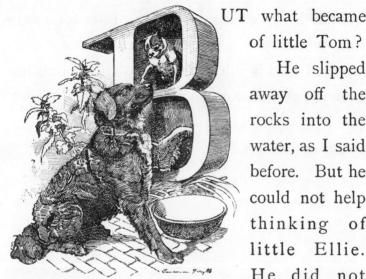

BUT what became of little Tom?

He slipped away off the rocks into the water, as I said before. But he could not help thinking of little Ellie. He did not remember who she was; but he knew that she was a little girl, though she was a hundred times as big as he, and he thought about her all that day, and longed to have had her to play with; but he had very soon to think of something else. And here is the account of what happened to him, as it was published next morning in the Waterproof Gazette, on the finest watered paper, for the use of the great fairy, Mrs. Bedonebyasyoudid, who reads the news very carefully every morning, and especially the police cases, as you will hear very soon.

He was going along the rocks in three-fathom water, watching the pollock catch prawns, when he saw a round cage of green withes; and inside it, looking very much ashamed of himself, sat his friend the lobster, twiddling his horns, instead of thumbs.

"What, have you been naughty, and have they put you in the lock-up?" asked Tom.

The lobster felt a little indignant at such a notion, but he was too much depressed in spirits to argue; so he only said, "I can't get out."

"Why did you get in?"

"After that nasty piece of dead fish." He had thought it looked and smelt very nice when he was outside, and so it did, for a lobster: but now he turned round and abused it because he was angry with himself.

"Where did you get in?"

"Through that round hole at the top."

"Then why don't you get out through it?"

"Because I can't": and the lobster twiddled his horns more fiercely than ever, but he was forced to confess.

"I have jumped upwards, downwards, backwards, and sideways, at least four thousand times; and I can't get out: I always get up underneath there, and can't find the hole."

Tom looked at the trap, and having more wit than the lobster, he saw plainly enough what was the matter; as you may if you will look at a lobster-pot.

"Stop a bit," said Tom. "Turn your tail

up to me, and I'll pull you through hindfore-most, and then you won't stick in the spikes."

But the lobster was so stupid and clumsy that he couldn't hit the hole.

Tom reached and clawed down the hole after him, till he caught hold of him; and then, as was to be expected, the clumsy lobster pulled him in head foremost.

"Hullo! here is a pretty business," said Tom. "Now take your great claws, and break the points off those spikes, and then we shall both get out easily."

"Dear me, I never thought of that," said the lobster; "and after all the experience of life that I have had!"

But they had not got half the spikes away when they saw a great dark cloud over them: and lo, and behold, it was the otter.

How she did grin and grin when she saw Tom. "Yar!" said she, "you little meddlesome wretch, I have you now! I will serve you out for telling the salmon where I was!" And she crawled all over the pot to get in.

Tom was horribly frightened, and still more frightened when she found the hole in the top, and squeezed herself right down through it, all eyes and teeth. But no sooner was her head inside than valiant Mr. Lobster caught her by the nose and held on.

And there they were all three in the pot, rolling over and over, and very tight packing it was. And the lobster tore at the otter, and the otter tore at the lobster, and both squeezed and thumped poor Tom till he had no breath left in his body; and I don't know what would have happened to him if he had not at last got on the otter's back, and safe out of the hole.

He was right glad when he got out: but he would not desert his friend who had saved him; and the first time he saw his tail uppermost he caught hold of it, and pulled with all his might.

But the lobster would not let go.

"Come along," said Tom; "don't you see she is dead?" And so she was, quite drowned and dead.

And that was the end of the wicked otter.

But the lobster would not let go.

"Come along, you stupid old stick-in-the-mud," cried Tom, "or the fisherman will catch you!" And that was true, for Tom felt some one above beginning to haul up the pot.

But the lobster would not let go.

Tom saw the fisherman haul him up to the boat-side, and thought it was all up with him. But when Mr. Lobster saw the fisherman, he gave such a furious and tremendous snap, that he snapped out of his hand, and out of the pot, and safe into the sea. But he left his knobbed claw behind him; for it never came into his stupid head to let go after all, so he just shook his claw off as the easier method.

And now happened to Tom a most wonderful

THE **LOBSTER** SNAPPED OUT OF HIS HAND, AND OUT OF THE POT, AND
SAFE INTO THE SEA

thing; for he had not left the lobster five minutes before he came upon a water-baby.

A real live water-baby, sitting on the white sand, very busy about a little point of rock. And when it saw Tom it looked up for a moment, and then cried, " Why, you are not one of us. You are a new baby! Oh, how delightful!"

And it ran to Tom, and Tom ran to it, and they hugged and kissed each other for ever so long, they did not know why.

At last Tom said, " Oh, where have you been all this while? I have been looking for you so long, and I have been so lonely."

"We have been here for days and days. There are hundreds of us about the rocks. How was it you did not see us, or hear us when we sing and romp every evening before we go home?"

Tom looked at the baby again, and then he said:

"Well, this is wonderful! I have seen things

L

just like you again and again, but I thought you were shells, or sea-creatures. I never took you for water-babies like myself."

Now, was not that very odd? So odd, indeed, that you will, no doubt, want to know how it happened, and why Tom could never find a water-baby till after he had got the lobster out of the pot. And, if you will read this story nine times over, and then think for yourself, you will find out why.

"Now," said the baby, "come and help me, or I shall not have finished before my brothers and sisters come, and it is time to go home."

"What shall I help you at?"

"At this poor dear little rock; a great clumsy boulder came rolling by in the last storm, and knocked all its head off, and rubbed off all its flowers. And now I must plant it again with seaweeds, and coralline, and anemones, and I will make it the prettiest little rock-garden on all the shore."

So they worked away at the rock, and planted it, and smoothed the sand down round it, and capital fun they had till the tide began to turn. And then Tom heard all the other babies coming, laughing and singing and shouting and romping; and the noise they made was just like the noise of the ripple. So he knew that he had been hearing and seeing the water-babies all along; only he did not know them, because his eyes and ears were not opened.

And in they came, dozens and dozens of them, some bigger than Tom and some smaller, all in the neatest little white bathing dresses; and when they found that he was a new baby, they hugged him and kissed him, and then put him in the middle and danced round him on the sand, and there was no one ever so happy as poor little Tom.

"Now then," they cried all at once, "we must come away home, we must come away home, or the tide will leave us dry. We have mended all the broken seaweed, and put all the rock-pools in order, and planted all the shells again in the sand, and nobody will see where the ugly storm swept in last week."

And this is the reason why the rock-pools are always so neat and clean; because the water-babies come inshore after every storm to sweep them out, and comb them down, and put them all to rights again.

CHAPTER XI

THE HOME OF THE WATER-BABIES AND MRS. BEDONEBYASYOUDID

AND where is the home of the water-babies? In St. Brandan's fairy isle.

Now when Tom got there, he found that the isle stood all on pillars, and that its roots were full of caves. There were pillars of black basalt, like Staffa; and pillars of green and crimson serpentine, like Kynance; and pillars ribboned with red and white and yellow sandstone, like Livermead; and there were blue grottoes like Capri, and white grottoes like Adelsberg; all curtained and draped with seaweeds, purple and crimson, green and brown; and strewn with soft white sand, on which the water-babies sleep every night. But, to keep the place clean and

sweet, the crabs picked up all the scraps off the
floor and ate them like so many monkeys; while
the rocks were covered with ten thousand sea-
anemones, and corals and madrepores, who
scavenged the water all day long, and kept it
nice and pure. But, to make up to them for
having to do such nasty work, they were not
left black and dirty, as poor chimney-sweeps
and dustmen are. No; the fairies are more
considerate and just than that, and have dressed
them all in the most beautiful colours and
patterns, till they look like vast flower-beds of
gay blossoms.

And, instead of watchmen and policemen to
keep out nasty things at night, there were
thousands and thousands of water-snakes, and
most wonderful creatures they were. They
were all named after the sea-fairies who took
care of them. They were dressed in green
velvet, and black velvet, and purple velvet;
and were all jointed in rings; and some had

eyes in their tails ; and some had eyes in every joint, so that they kept a very sharp look-out ; and when they wanted a baby-snake, they just grew one at the end of their own tails, and when it was able to take care of itself it dropped off ; so that they brought up their families very cheaply. But if any nasty thing came by, out they rushed upon it ; and then out of each of their hundreds of feet there sprang a whole cutler's shop of

Scythes,	*Billhooks,*	*Pickaxes,*
Forks,	*Penknives,*	*Swords,*
Lances,	*Fishhooks,*	*Gimblets,*
Corkscrews,	*Pins,*	*Needles,*
	And so forth,	

which stabbed, shot, poked, pricked, scratched, ripped, pinked, and crimped those naughty beasts so terribly that they had to run for their lives, or else be chopped into small pieces and be eaten afterwards.

And there were the water-babies in thousands, more than Tom, or you either, could count.

But I wish Tom had given up all his naughty tricks, and left off tormenting dumb animals now that he had plenty of playfellows to amuse him. Instead of that, I am sorry to say, he would meddle with the creatures, all but the water-snakes, for they would stand no nonsense. So he tickled the madrepores, to make them shut up; and frightened the crabs, to make them hide in the sand and peep out at him with the tips of their eyes; and put stones into the anemones' mouths, to make them fancy that their dinner was coming.

The other children warned him, and said, "Take care what you are at. Mrs. Bedonebyasyoudid is coming." But Tom never heeded them, being quite riotous with high spirits and good luck, till, one Friday morning early, Mrs. Bedonebyasyoudid came indeed.

A very tremendous lady she was; and when

the children saw her they all stood in a row,
very upright indeed, and smoothed down their
bathing dresses, and put their hands behind
them, just as if they were going to be examined
by the inspector.

And she had on a black bonnet, and a black
shawl; and a pair of large green spectacles,
and a great hooked nose, hooked so much that
the bridge of it stood quite up above her eye-
brows; and under her arm she carried a great
birch-rod. Indeed, she was so ugly that Tom
was tempted to make faces at her: but did not;
for he did not admire the look of the birch-rod
under her arm.

And she looked at the children one by one,
and seemed very much pleased with them, though
she never asked them one question about how
they were behaving; and then began giving
them all sorts of nice sea-things—sea-cakes, sea-
apples, sea-oranges, sea-bullseyes, sea-toffee;
and to the very best of all she gave sea-ices,

made out of sea-cows' cream, which never melt
under water.

Now little Tom watched all these sweet
things given away, till his mouth watered, and
his eyes grew as round as an owl's. For he
hoped that his turn would come at last; and so
it did. For the lady called him up, and held
out her fingers with something in them, and
popped it into his mouth; and, lo and behold,
it was a nasty cold hard pebble.

"You are a very cruel woman," said he, and
began to whimper.

"And you are a very cruel boy; who puts
pebbles into the sea-anemones' mouths, to take
them in, and make them fancy that they had
caught a good dinner! As you did to them,
so I must do to you."

"Who told you that?" said Tom.

"You did yourself, this very minute."

Tom had never opened his lips; so he was
very much taken aback indeed.

"Yes; every one tells me exactly what they have done wrong; and that without knowing

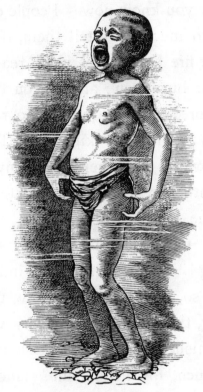

it themselves. So there is no use trying to hide anything from me. Now go, and be a good boy, and I will put no more pebbles in your mouth, if you put none in other creatures'."

"I did not know there was any harm in it," said Tom.

"Then you know now. People continually say that to me : but I tell them, if you don't know that fire burns, that is no reason that it should not burn you ; and if you don't know that dirt breeds fever, that is no reason why the fevers should not kill you. The lobster did not know that there was any harm in getting into the lobster-pot ; but it caught him all the same."

"Dear me," thought Tom, "she knows everything !" And so she did, indeed.

"And so, if you do not know that things are wrong, that is no reason why you should not be punished for them ; though not as much, not as much, my little man" (and the lady looked very kindly, after all), "as if you did know."

"Well, you are a little hard on a poor lad," said Tom.

"Not at all; I am the best friend you ever had in all your life. But I will tell you; I cannot help punishing people when they do wrong. I like it no more than they do; I am often very, very sorry for them, poor things: but I cannot help it. If I tried not to do it, I should do it all the same. For I work by machinery, just like an engine; and am full of wheels and springs inside; and am wound up very carefully, so that I cannot help going."

"Was it long ago since they wound you up?" asked Tom. For he thought, the cunning little fellow, "She will run down some day: or they may forget to wind her up, as old Grimes used to forget to wind up his watch when he came in from the public-house; and then I shall be safe."

"I was wound up once and for all, so long ago, that I forget all about it."

"Dear me," said Tom, "you must have been made a long time!"

"I never was made, my child; and I shall go for ever and ever."

And there came over the lady's face a very curious expression—very solemn, and very sad; and yet very, very sweet. And she looked up and away, as if she were gazing through the sea, and through the sky, at something far, far off; and as she did so, there came such a quiet, tender, patient, hopeful smile over her face that Tom thought for the moment that she did not look ugly at all.

And Tom smiled in her face, she looked so pleasant for the moment. And the strange fairy smiled too, and said:

"Yes. You thought me very ugly just now, did you not?"

Tom hung down his head, and got very red about the ears.

"And I am very ugly. I am the ugliest fairy in the world; and I shall be, till people behave themselves as they ought to do. And then I shall grow as handsome as my sister, who is the loveliest fairy in the world; and her name is Mrs. Doasyouwouldbedoneby. So she begins where I end, and I begin where she ends; and those who will not listen to her must listen to me, as you will see. Now, all of you run away, except Tom; and he may stay and see what I am going to do. It will be a very good warning for him to begin with, before he goes to school.

"Now, Tom, every Friday I come down here and call up all who have ill-used little children and serve them as they served the children."

And at that Tom was frightened, and crept under a stone; which made the two crabs who lived there very angry.

"These people," she said, "did not know that they were doing wrong: they were only stupid and impatient; and therefore I only punish them till they become patient, and learn to use their common sense like reasonable beings. And now do you be a good boy, and do as you would be done by, which they did not; and then, when my sister, MADAME DO-ASYOUWOULDBEDONEBY, comes on Sunday, perhaps she will take notice of you, and teach you how to behave. She understands that better than I do." And so she went.

Tom determined to be a very good boy all Saturday; and he was; for he never frightened one crab, nor tickled any live corals, nor put stones into the sea anemones' mouths, to make them fancy they had got a dinner; and when Sunday morning came, sure enough, MRS. DO-ASYOUWOULDBEDONEBY came too. Whereat all the little children began dancing and clapping their hands, and Tom danced too with all his might.

And as for the pretty lady, I cannot tell you what the colour of her hair was, or of her eyes: no more could Tom; for, when any one

looks at her, all they can think of is, that she
has the sweetest, kindest, tenderest, funniest,

merriest face they ever saw, or want to see.
But Tom saw that she was a very tall woman,
as tall as her sister; and she understood babies
thoroughly, for she had plenty of her own, whole

M

rows and regiments of them, and has to this day. And all her delight was, whenever she had a spare moment, to play with babies; for babies are the best company, and the pleasantest playfellows, in the world. And therefore when the children saw her, they naturally all caught hold of her, and pulled her till she sat down on a stone, and climbed into her lap, and clung round her neck, and caught hold of her hands; and then they all put their thumbs into their mouths, and began cuddling and purring like so many kittens, as they ought to have done. While those who could get nowhere else sat down on the sand, and cuddled her feet—for no one, you know, wears shoes in the water. And Tom stood staring at them; for he could not understand what it was all about.

"And who are you, you little darling?" she said.

"Oh, that is the new baby!" they all cried, pulling their thumbs out of their mouths; "and

he never had any mother," and they all put
their thumbs back again, for they did not wish
to lose any time.

"Then I will be his mother, and he shall
have the very best place; so get out, all of you,
this moment."

And she took up two great armfuls of babies
—nine hundred under one arm, and thirteen
hundred under the other—and threw them
away, right and left, into the water. They did
not mind, but came paddling and wriggling
back to her like so many tadpoles, till you
could see nothing of her from head to foot for
the swarm of little babies.

But she took Tom in her arms, and laid
him in the softest place of all, and kissed him,
and patted him, and talked to him, tenderly
and low, such things as he had never heard
before in his life; and Tom looked up into her
eyes, and loved her, and loved, till he fell fast
asleep from pure love.

And when he woke she was telling the children a story. And what story did she tell them? One story she told them, which begins every Christmas Eve, and yet never ends at all for ever and ever; and, as she went on, the children took their thumbs out of their mouths and listened quite seriously; but not sadly at all; for she never told them anything sad; and Tom listened too, and never grew tired of listening. And he listened so long that he fell fast asleep again, and, when he woke, the lady was nursing him still.

"Don't go away," said little Tom. "This is so nice. I never had any one to cuddle me before."

"Don't go away," said all the children; "you have not sung us one song."

"Well, I have time for only one. So what shall it be?"

"The doll you lost! The doll you lost!" cried all the babies at once.

So the strange fairy sang :—

I once had a sweet little doll, dears,
The prettiest doll in the world ;
Her cheeks were so red and so white, dears,
And her hair was so charmingly curled.
But I lost my poor little doll, dears,
As I played in the heath one day ;
And I cried for her more than a week, dears,
But I never could find where she lay.

I found my poor little doll, dears,
As I played in the heath one day :
Folks say she is terribly changed, dears,
For her paint is all washed away,
And her arm trodden off by the cows, dears,
And her hair not the least bit curled :
Yet, for old sakes' sake she is still, dears,
The prettiest doll in the world.

"Now," said the fairy to Tom, "will you be a good boy for my sake, and torment no more sea-beasts till I come back?"

"And you will cuddle me again?" said poor little Tom.

"Of course I will, you little duck. I should like to take you with me and cuddle you all the way, only I must not"; and away she went.

So Tom really tried to be a good boy, and tormented no sea-beasts after that as long as he lived; and he is quite alive, I assure you, still.

Oh, how good little boys ought to be who have kind mammas to cuddle them and tell them stories; and how afraid they ought to be of growing naughty, and bringing tears into their mammas' pretty eyes!

CHAPTER XII

Now you may fancy that Tom was quite
good, when he had everything that he could
want or wish: but you would be very much
mistaken. Being quite comfortable is a very
good thing; but it does not make people good.
Indeed, it sometimes makes them naughty, and
I am very sorry to say that this happened to
little Tom. For he grew so fond of the sea-
bullseyes and sea-lollipops that his foolish little
head could think of nothing else: and he was
always longing for more, and wondering when
the strange lady would come again and give
him some, and what she would give him, and
how much, and whether she would give him
more than the others. And he thought of

nothing but lollipops by day, and dreamt of nothing else by night—and what happened then?

That he began to watch the lady to see where she kept the sweet things: and began hiding, and sneaking, and following her about, and pretending to be looking the other way, or going after something else, till he found out that she kept them in a beautiful mother-of-pearl cabinet away in a deep crack of the rocks.

And he longed to go to the cabinet, and yet he was afraid; and then he longed again, and was less afraid; and at last, by continual thinking about it, he longed so violently that he was not afraid at all. And one night, when all the other children were asleep, and he could not sleep for thinking of lollipops, he crept away among the rocks, and got to the cabinet, and behold! it was open.

But, when he saw all the nice things inside, instead of being delighted, he was quite frightened, and wished he had never come there. And then he would only touch them, and he did; and then he would only taste one, and he did; and then he would only eat one, and he did; and then he would only eat two, and then three, and so on; and then he was terrified lest she should come and catch him, and began gobbling them down so fast that he did not taste them, or have any pleasure in them; and then he felt sick, and would have only one more; and then only one more again; and so on till he had eaten them all up.

And all the while, close behind him, stood Mrs. Bedonebyasyoudid.

She took off her spectacles, because she did not like to see too much, and her eyes filled with great big tears, but all she said was:

"Ah, you poor little dear! you are just like all the rest."

But she said it to herself, and Tom neither heard nor saw her.

But what did the strange fairy do when she saw all her lollipops eaten?

She just said nothing at all about the matter, not even when Tom came next day with the rest for sweet things. He was horribly afraid of coming: but he was still more afraid of staying away, lest any one should suspect him. He was dreadfully afraid, too, lest there should be no sweets—as was to be expected, he having eaten them all—and lest then the fairy should inquire who had taken them. But, behold! she pulled out just as many as ever, which astonished Tom, and frightened him still more.

And, when the fairy looked him full in the face, he shook from head to foot: however, she gave him his share like the rest, and he thought within himself that she could not have found him out.

But, when he put the sweets into his mouth, he hated the taste of them; and they made him so sick that he had to get away as fast as he could; and terribly sick he was, and very cross and unhappy, all the week after.

Then, when next week came, he had his share again; and again the fairy looked him full in the face; but more sadly than she had ever looked. And he could not bear the sweets: but took them again in spite of himself.

And when Mrs. Doasyouwouldbedoneby came, he wanted to be cuddled like the rest; but she said very seriously:

"I should like to cuddle you; but I cannot, you are so horny and prickly."

And Tom looked at himself: and he was all over prickles, just like a sea-hedgehog.

Which was quite natural; for you must know and believe that people's souls make their bodies just as a snail makes its shell. And therefore, when Tom's soul grew all prickly with naughty tempers, his body could not help growing prickly too, so that nobody would cuddle him, or play with him, or even like to look at him.

What could Tom do now but go away and hide in a corner and cry? For nobody would play with him, and he knew full well why.

And he was so miserable all that week that when the ugly fairy came and looked at him once more full in the face, more seriously and sadly than ever, he could stand it no longer, and thrust the sweetmeats away, saying, "No, I don't want any: I can't bear them now," and then burst out crying, poor little man, and told Mrs. Bedonebyasyoudid every word as it happened.

He was horribly frightened when he had done so; for he expected her to punish him very severely. But, instead, she only took him up and kissed him.

"I will forgive you, little man," she said. "I always forgive every one the moment they tell me the truth of their own accord."

"Then you will take away all these nasty prickles?"

"That is a very different matter.   You put

them there yourself, and only you can take them away."

"But how can I do that?" asked Tom, crying afresh.

"Well, I think it is time for you to go to school; so I shall fetch you a schoolmistress, who will teach you how to get rid of your prickles." And so she went away.

Tom was frightened at the notion of a schoolmistress; for he thought she would certainly come with a birch-rod or a cane; but he comforted himself, at last, with thinking that she might be something like the old woman in Vendale—which she was not in the least; for, when the fairy brought her, she was the most beautiful little girl that ever was seen, with long curls floating behind her like a golden cloud, and long robes floating all round her like a silver one.

"There he is," said the fairy; "and you must teach him to be good, whether you like or not."

"I know," said the little girl; but she did not seem quite to like, for she put her finger in her mouth, and looked at Tom under her brows; and Tom put his finger in his mouth, and looked at her under his brows, for he was horribly ashamed of himself.

The little girl seemed hardly to know how to begin; and perhaps she would never have begun at all if poor Tom had not burst out crying, and begged her to teach him to be good and help him to cure his prickles; and at that she grew so tender-hearted that she began teaching him as prettily as ever child was taught in the world.

And what did the little girl teach Tom? She taught him, first, what you have been taught ever since you said your first prayers at your mother's knees.

She taught Tom every day in the week; only on Sundays she always went away home, and the kind fairy took her place. And before she had taught Tom many Sundays, his prickles had vanished quite away, and his skin was smooth and clean again.

"Dear me!" said the little girl; "why, I know you now. You are the very same little chimney-sweep who came into my bedroom."

"Dear me!" cried Tom. "And I know you, too, now. You are the very little white lady whom I saw in bed." And he jumped at her, and longed to hug and kiss her; but did not, remembering that she was a lady born; so he only jumped round and round her till he was quite tired.

And then they began telling each other all their story—how he had got into the water, and she had fallen over the rock; and how he had swum down to the sea, and how she had flown out of the window; and how this, that, and the other, till it was all talked out: and then they both began over again, and I can't say which of the two talked fastest.

And then they set to work at their lessons again, and both liked them so well that they went on well till seven full years were past and gone.

TOM BEGGED HER TO TEACH HIM TO BE GOOD AND HELP HIM TO
CURE HIS PRICKLES

You may fancy that Tom was quite content and happy all those seven years; but the truth is, he was not. He had always one thing on his mind, and that was—where little Ellie went, when she went home on Sundays.

To a very beautiful place, she said.

But what was the beautiful place like, and where was it ?

Ah! that is just what she could not say, save that it is the most beautiful place in all the world, and that it was worth all the rest of the world put together. And of course that only made Tom the more anxious to go likewise.

"Miss Ellie," he said at last, "I will know why I cannot go with you when you go home on Sundays, or I shall have no peace, and give you none either."

"You must ask the fairies that."

So when the fairy, Mrs. Bedonebyasyoudid, came next, Tom asked her.

N

"Little boys who are only fit to play with sea-beasts cannot go there," she said. "Those who go there must go first where they do not like, and do what they do not like, and help somebody they do not like."

"Why, did Ellie do that?"

"Ask her."

And Ellie blushed, and said, "Yes, Tom; I did not like coming here at first; I was so much happier at home, where it is always Sunday. And I was afraid of you, Tom, at first, because—because——"

"Because I was all over prickles? But I am not prickly now, am I, Miss Ellie?"

"No," said Ellie. "I like you very much now; and I like coming here, too."

"And perhaps," said the fairy, "you will learn to like going where you don't like, and helping some one that you don't like, as Ellie has."

But Tom put his finger in his mouth, and

hung his head down ; for he did not see that at all.

So when Mrs. Doasyouwouldbedoneby came, Tom asked her ; for he thought in his little head, She is not so strict as her sister, and perhaps she may let me off more easily.

But when he asked the second fairy, she told him just what the first did, and in the very same words.

Tom was very unhappy at that. And, when Ellie went home on Sunday, he fretted and cried all day, and did not care to listen to the fairy's stories about good children, though they were prettier than ever. Indeed, the more he overheard of them, the less he liked to listen, because they were all about children who did what they did not like, and took trouble for other people, and worked to feed their little brothers and sisters instead of caring only for their play. And, when she began to tell a story about a holy child in old times, who was martyred by the heathen because it would not worship idols, Tom could bear no more, and ran away and hid among the rocks.

And, when Ellie came back, he was shy with her, because he fancied she looked down on him, and thought him a coward. And then he grew quite cross with her, because she was superior to him, and did what he could not do. And poor Ellie was quite surprised and sad; and at last Tom burst out crying; but he would not tell her what was really in his mind.

And all the while he was eaten up with curiosity to know where Ellie went to; so that he began not to care for his playmates, or for the sea-palace or anything else. But perhaps that made matters all the easier for him; for he grew so discontented with everything round him that he did not care to stay, and did not care where he went.

"Well," he said, at last, "I am so miserable here, I'll go; if only you will go with me?"

"Ah!" said Ellie, "I wish I might; but the worst of it is, that the fairy says that you must go alone if you go at all. Now don't poke that poor crab about, Tom" (for he was feeling very naughty and mischievous), "or the fairy will have to punish you."

Tom was very nearly saying, "I don't care if she does"; but he stopped himself in time.

"I know what she wants me to do," he said, whining most dolefully. "She wants me to go after that horrid old Grimes. I don't like him, that's certain. And if I find him, he will turn me into a chimney-sweep again, I know. That's what I have been afraid of all along."

"No, he won't—I know as much as that. Nobody can turn water-babies into sweeps, or hurt them at all, as long as they are good."

"Ah," said naughty Tom, "I see what you

want; you are persuading me all along to go, because you are tired of me, and want to get rid of me."

Little Ellie opened her eyes very wide at that, and they were all brimming over with tears.

"Oh, Tom, Tom!" she said, very mournfully—and then she cried, "Oh, Tom! where are you?"

And Tom cried, "Oh, Ellie, where are you?"

For neither of them could see each other— not the least. Little Ellie vanished quite away, and Tom heard her voice calling him, and growing smaller and smaller, and fainter and fainter, till all was silent.

Who was frightened then but Tom? He swam up and down among the rocks, into all the halls and chambers, faster than ever he swam before, but could not find her. He shouted after her, but she did not answer; he

asked all the other children, but they had not
seen her; and at last he went up to the top

of the water and began crying and screaming
for Mrs. Bedonebyasyoudid—which perhaps was
the best thing to do—for she came in a moment.

"Oh!" said Tom. "Oh dear, oh dear! I have been naughty to Ellie, and I have killed her—I know I have killed her."

"Not quite that," said the fairy; "but I have sent her away home, and she will not come back again for I do not know how long."

And at that Tom cried bitterly.

"How cruel of you to send Ellie away!" sobbed Tom. "However, I will find her again, if I go to the world's end to look for her."

The fairy did not slap Tom, and tell him to hold his tongue: but she took him on her lap very kindly, just as her sister would have done; and put him in mind how it was not her fault, because she was wound up inside, like watches, and could not help doing things whether she liked or not. And then she told him how he had been in the nursery long enough, and must go out now and see the world, if he intended ever to be a man; and how he must go all alone by himself, as every one else that ever was born has to go, and see with his own eyes, and smell with his own nose, and make his own bed and lie on it, and burn his own fingers if he put them into the fire. And then she told him how many fine things there were to be seen in the world, and what sort of a place it was, and then she told him not to be afraid of anything he met, for nothing would harm him if he remembered all his lessons, and did what he knew was right. And at last she comforted poor little Tom so much that he was quite eager to go, and wanted to set out that minute. "Only," he said, "if I might see Ellie once before I went!"

"Why do you want that?"

"Because—because I should be so much happier if I thought she had forgiven me."

And in the twinkling of an eye there stood Ellie, smiling, and looking so happy that Tom longed to kiss her; but was still afraid it would not be respectful, because she was a lady born.

"I am going, Ellie!" said Tom. "I am going, if it is to the world's end. But I don't like going at all, and that's the truth."

"Pooh! pooh! pooh!" said the fairy. "You will like it very well indeed, you little rogue, and you know that at the bottom of your heart. But if you don't, I will make you like it. Come here, and see what happens to people who do only what is pleasant."

And she took out of one of her cupboards (she had all sorts of mysterious cupboards in the cracks of the rocks) the most wonderful waterproof book, full of such photographs as never were seen.

CHAPTER XIII

THE STORY OF THE DOASYOULIKES

THE children looked with great delight for the opening of the book.

And on the title-page was written, "The History of the great and famous nation of the Doasyoulikes, who came away from the country of Hardwork, because they wanted to play on the Jews' harp all day long."

In the first picture they saw these Doasyoulikes living in the land of Readymade, at the foot of the Happy-go-lucky Mountains, where flapdoodle grows wild; and if you want to know what that is, you must read Peter Simple.

Instead of houses they lived in the beautiful caves of tufa, and bathed in the warm springs three times a day; and, as for clothes, it was so warm there that the gentlemen walked about in little beside a cocked hat and a pair of straps, or some light summer tackle of that kind; and the ladies all gathered gossamer in autumn (when they were not too lazy) to make their winter dresses.

They were very fond of music, but it was too much trouble to learn the piano or the violin; and as for dancing, that would have been too great an exertion. So they sat on ant-hills all day long, and played on the Jews' harp; and, if the ants bit them, why they just got up and went to the next ant-hill, till they were bitten there likewise.

And they sat under the flapdoodle-trees, and let the flapdoodle drop into their mouths; and under the vines, and squeezed the grape-juice down their throats; and, if any little pigs ran about ready roasted, crying, "Come and eat me," as was their fashion in that country, they waited till the pigs ran against their mouths, and then took a bite, and were content, just as so many oysters would have been.

They needed no weapons, for no enemies ever came near their land; and no tools, for everything was readymade to their hand; and the stern old fairy Necessity never came near them to hunt them up, and make them use their wits, or die.

And so on, and so on, and so on, till there were never such comfortable, easy-going, happy-go-lucky people in the world.

"Well, that is a jolly life," said Tom.

"You think so?" said the fairy. "Do you see that great peaked mountain there behind," said the fairy, "with smoke coming out of its top?"

"Yes."

"And do you see all those ashes, and slag, and cinders lying about?"

"Yes."

"Then turn over the next five hundred years, and you will see what happens next."

And behold the mountain had blown up like a barrel of gunpowder, and then boiled over like a kettle; whereby one-third of the Doasyoulikes were blown into the air, and another third were smothered in ashes; so that there was only one-third left.

"You see," said the fairy, "what comes of living on a burning mountain."

"Oh, why did you not warn them?" said little Ellie.

"I did warn them all that I could. I let the smoke come out of the mountain; and wherever there is smoke there is fire. And I laid the ashes and cinders all about; and wherever there are cinders, cinders may be again. But they did not like to face facts, my dears, as very few people do; and so they invented a cock-and-bull story, which, I am sure, I never told them, that the smoke was the breath of a giant, whom some gods or other had buried under the mountain ; and that the cinders were what the dwarfs roasted the little pigs whole with ; and other nonsense of that kind. And, when folks are in that humour, I cannot teach them, save by the good old birch-rod." And then she turned over the next five hundred years : and there were the remnant of the Doasyoulikes, doing as they liked, as before. They were too lazy to move away from the mountain ; so they said, If it has blown up once, that is all the more reason that it should not blow up again. And they were few in number : but they only said, The more the merrier, but the fewer the better fare. However, that was not quite true ; for all the flapdoodle-trees were killed by the volcano, and they had eaten all the roast pigs, who, of course, could not be expected to have little ones. So they had to live very hard, on nuts and roots which they scratched out of the ground with sticks. Some of them talked of sowing corn, as their ancestors used to do, before they came into the land of Readymade; but they had forgotten how to make ploughs (they had forgotten even how to make Jews' harps by this time), and had eaten all the seed-corn which they brought out of the land of Hardwork years since; and of course it was too much trouble to go away and find more. So they lived miserably on roots and nuts, and all the weakly little children had great stomachs, and then died.

"Why," said Tom, "they are growing no better than savages."

"And look how ugly they are all getting," said Ellie.

"Yes; when people live on poor vegetables instead of roast beef and plum-pudding, their jaws grow large, and their lips grow coarse."

And she turned over the next five hundred

AN EFT IN A POND

years. And there they were all living up in trees, and making nests to keep off the rain. And underneath the trees lions were prowling about.

"Why," said Ellie, "the lions seem to have eaten a good many of them, for there are very few left now."

"Yes," said the fairy; "you see it was only the strongest and most active ones who could climb the trees, and so escape."

"But what great, hulking, broad-shouldered chaps they are," said Tom; "they are a rough lot as ever I saw."

"Yes, they are getting very strong now; for the ladies will not marry any but the very strongest and fiercest gentlemen, who can help them up the trees out of the lions' way."

And she turned over the next five hundred years. And in that they were fewer still, and stronger, and fiercer; but their feet had changed shape very oddly, for they laid hold of the

o

branches with their great toes, as if they had been thumbs, just as a Hindoo tailor uses his toes to thread his needle.

The children were very much surprised, and asked the fairy whether that was her doing.

"Yes, and no," she said, smiling. "It was only those who could use their feet as well as their hands who could get a good living: or, indeed, get married; so that they got the best of everything, and starved out all the rest; and those who are left keep up a regular breed of toe-thumb-men."

"But there is a hairy one among them," said Ellie.

"Ah!" said the fairy, "that will be a great man in his time, and chief of all the tribe."

And, when she turned over the next five hundred years, it was true.

For this hairy chief had had hairy children, and they hairier children still; and every one

wished to marry hairy husbands, and have
hairy children too; for the climate was growing

so damp that none but the hairy ones could
live: all the rest coughed and sneezed, and
had sore throats, and went into consumptions,

before they could grow up to be men and women.

Then the fairy turned over the next five hundred years. And they were fewer still.

"Why, there is one on the ground picking up roots," said Ellie, "and he cannot walk upright."

No more he could; for in the same way that the shape of their feet had altered, the shape of their backs had altered also.

"Why," cried Tom, "I declare they are all apes."

"Something fearfully like it, poor foolish creatures," said the fairy. "They are grown so stupid now, that they can hardly think: for none of them have used their wits for many hundred years. They have almost forgotten, too, how to talk. For each stupid child forgot some of the words it heard from its stupid parents, and had not wits enough to make fresh words for itself. Beside, they are grown so fierce and suspicious and brutal that they keep out of each other's way, and mope and sulk in the dark forests, never hearing each other's voice, till they have forgotten almost what speech is like. I am afraid they will all be apes very soon, and all by doing only what they liked."

And in the next five hundred years they were all dead and gone, by bad food and wild beasts and hunters.

And that was the end of the great and jolly nation of the Doasyoulikes. And, when Tom and Ellie came to the end of the book, they looked very sad and solemn; and they had good reason so to do.

"But could you not have saved them from becoming apes?" said little Ellie, at last.

"At first, my dear; if only they would have behaved like men, and set to work to do what they did not like. But the longer they waited, and behaved like the dumb beasts, who only do what they like, the stupider and clumsier they grew; till at last they were past all cure, for they had thrown their own wits away. It is such things as this that help to make me so ugly, that I know not when I shall grow fair."

"And where are they all now?" asked Ellie.

"Exactly where they ought to be, my dear.

"Yes!" said the fairy, solemnly, half to herself, as she closed the wonderful book. "Folks say now that I can make beasts into men. Well, perhaps they are right; and perhaps, again, they are wrong. That is one of the seven things which I am forbidden to tell; and, at all events, it is no concern of theirs. Whatever their ancestors were, men they are; and I advise them to behave as such, and act accordingly. But let them recollect this, that there are two sides to every question, and a downhill as well as an uphill road; and, if I can turn beasts into men, I can, by the same laws, turn men into beasts. You were very near being turned into a beast once or twice, little Tom. Indeed, if you had not made up your mind to go on this journey, and see the world, like an Englishman, I am not sure but that you would have ended as an eft in a pond."

"Oh, dear me!" said Tom; "sooner than that, and be all over slime, I'll go this minute, if it is to the world's end."

CHAPTER XIV

TOM'S JOURNEY TO SHINY WALL

And Nature, the old Nurse, took
  The child upon her knee,
Saying, "Here is a story book
  " Thy father hath written for thee.

"Come wander with me," she said,
  " Into regions yet untrod,

And read what is still unread
  In the Manuscripts of God."

And he wandered away and away
  With Nature, the dear old Nurse,
Who sang to him night and day
  The rhymes of the universe.
                 LONGFELLOW.

OW," said Tom, "I am ready to be off, if it's to the world's end."

"Ah!" said the fairy, "that is a brave, good boy. But you must go farther than the world's end, if you want to find Mr.

Grimes; for he is at the Other-end-of-Nowhere.
You must go to Shiny Wall, and through the
white gate that never was opened; and then
you will come to Peacepool, and Mother
Carey's Haven, where the good whales go when
they die. And there Mother Carey will tell
you the way to the Other-end-of-Nowhere, and
there you will find Mr. Grimes."

"Oh, dear!" said Tom. "But I do not
know my way to Shiny Wall, or where it is
at all."

"Little boys must take the trouble to find
out things for themselves, or they will never
grow to be men; so that you must ask all the
beasts in the sea and the birds in the air, and
if you have been good to them, some of them
will tell you the way to Shiny Wall."

"Well," said Tom, "it will be a long
journey, so I had better start at once. Good-
bye, Miss Ellie; you know I am getting a big
boy, and I must go out and see the world."

"I know you must," said Ellie; "but you will not forget me, Tom. I shall wait here till you come."

And she shook hands with him, and bade him good-bye. Tom longed very much again to kiss her; but he thought it would not be respectful, considering she was a lady born; so he promised not to forget her.

He asked all the beasts in the sea, and all the birds in the air, but none of them knew the way to Shiny Wall. For why? He was still too far down south.

Then he met a ship, far larger than he had ever seen—a gallant ocean-steamer, with a long cloud of smoke trailing behind; and he wondered how she went on without sails, and swam up to her to see. A school of dolphins were running races round and round her, going three feet for her one, and Tom asked them the way to Shiny Wall: but they did not know. Then he tried to find out how she moved, and at last he saw her screw, and was so delighted with it that he played under her quarter all day, till he nearly had his nose knocked off by the fans, and thought it time to move. Then he watched the sailors upon deck, and the ladies, with their bonnets and parasols: but none of them could see him, because their eyes were not opened,—as, indeed, most people's eyes are not.

At last there came out into the quarter-gallery a very pretty lady, in deep black widow's weeds, and in her arms a baby. She leaned over the quarter-gallery, and looked back and back toward England far away; and as she looked she sang:

I

" *Soft soft wind, from out the sweet south sliding,*
Waft thy silver cloud-webs athwart the summer sea ;
Thin thin threads of mist on dewy fingers twining,
Weave a veil of dappled gauze to shade my babe and me.

II

" Deep deep Love, within thine own abyss abiding,
Pour Thyself abroad, O Lord, on earth and air and sea ;
Worn weary hearts within Thy holy temple hiding,
Shield from sorrow, sin, and shame my helpless babe and me."

Her voice was so soft and low, and the music of the air so sweet, that Tom could have listened to it all day. But as she held the baby over the gallery rail, to show it the dolphins leaping and the water gurgling in the ship's wake, lo! and behold, the baby saw Tom.

He was quite sure of that; for when their eyes met, the baby smiled and held out his hands; and Tom smiled and held out his hands too; and the baby kicked and leaped, as if it wanted to jump overboard to him.

"What do you see, my darling?" said the lady; and her eyes followed the baby's till she too caught sight of Tom, swimming about among the foam-beads below.

She gave a little shriek and start; and then she said, quite quietly, "Babies in the sea? Well, perhaps it is the happiest place for them"; and waved her hand to Tom, and cried, "Wait a little, darling, only a little: and perhaps we shall go with you and be at rest."

And at that an old nurse, all in black, came out and talked to her, and drew her in. And Tom turned away northward, sad and wondering; and watched the great steamer slide away into the dusk, and the lights on board peep out one by one, and die out again, and the long bar of smoke fade away into the evening mist, till all was out of sight.

And he swam northward again, day after day, till at last he met the King of the Herrings, with a curry-comb growing out of his nose, and a sprat in his mouth for a cigar, and asked him the way to Shiny Wall; so he bolted his sprat head foremost, and said:

"If I were you, young gentleman, I should

go to the Allalonestone, and ask the last of
the Gairfowl."

Tom asked his way to her, and the King of
the Herrings told him very kindly.

But just as Tom had thanked him and set off, he called after him: "Hi! I say, can you fly?"

"I never tried," says Tom. "Why?"

"Because, if you can, I should advise you to say nothing to the old lady about it. There; take a hint. Good-bye."

And away Tom went for seven days and seven nights due north-west, till he came to a great codbank, the like of which he never saw before. The great cod lay below in tens of thousands, and gobbled shell-fish all day long; and the blue sharks roved above in hundreds, and gobbled them when they came up. So they ate, and ate, and ate each other, as they had done since the making of the world; for no man had come here yet to catch them, and find out how rich old Mother Carey is.

And there he saw the last of the Gairfowl, standing up on the Allalonestone, all alone. And a very grand old lady she was, full three feet high, and bolt upright, like some old Highland chieftainess. She had on a black velvet gown, and a white pinner and apron, and a very high bridge to her nose (which is a sure mark of high breeding), and a large pair of white spectacles on it, which made her look rather odd: but it was the ancient fashion of her house.

And instead of wings, she had two little feathery arms, with which she fanned herself, and complained of the dreadful heat; and she kept on crooning an old song to herself, which she learnt when she was a little baby-bird, long ago—

" Two little birds they sat on a stone,
One swam away, and then there was one,
With a fal-lal-la-lady.

" The other swam after, and then there was none,
And so the poor stone was left all alone ;
With a fal-lal-la-lady."

It was "flew" away, properly, and not "swam" away : but, as she could not fly, she

THE KING OF THE HERRINGS, WITH A SPRAT IN HIS MOUTH
FOR A CIGAR

had a right to alter it. However, it was a very fit song for her to sing, because she was a lady herself.

Tom came up to her very humbly, and made his bow; and the first thing she said was—

"Have you wings? Can you fly?"

"Oh dear, no, ma'am; I should not think of such a thing," said cunning little Tom.

"Then I shall have great pleasure in talking to you, my dear. It is quite refreshing nowadays to see anything without wings. They must all have wings, forsooth, now, every new upstart sort of bird, and fly. What can they want with flying, and raising themselves above their proper station in life? In the days of my ancestors no birds ever thought of having wings, and did very well without; and now they all laugh at me because I keep to the good old fashion."

And so she was running on, while Tom

P

tried to get in a word edgeways; and at last he did, when the old lady got out of breath, and began fanning herself again; and then he asked if she knew the way to Shiny Wall.

"Shiny Wall? Who should know better than I? We all came from Shiny Wall, thousands of years ago, when it was decently cold, and the climate was fit for gentlefolk; but now, I am the last of my family. A friend of mine and I came and settled on this rock when we were young, to be out of the way of low people. Once we were a great nation, and spread over all the Northern Isles. But men shot us so, and knocked us on the head, and took our eggs, until at last there were none of us left, except on the old Gairfowl-skerry, just off the Iceland coast, up which no man could climb. Even there we had no peace; for one day, when I was quite a young girl, the land rocked, and the sea boiled, and the sky grew dark, and all the air was filled with smoke and dust, and down tumbled the old Gairfowlskerry into the sea. The dovekies and marrocks, of course, all flew away; but we were too proud to do that. Some of us were dashed to pieces, and some drowned; and those who were left got away to Eldey, and the dovekies tell me they are all dead now, and so here I am left alone. And soon I shall be gone, my little dear, and nobody will miss me; and then the poor stone will be left all alone."

"But, please, which is the way to Shiny Wall?" said Tom.

"Oh, you must go, my little dear—you must go. Let me see—I am sure—that is— really, my poor old brains are getting quite puzzled. Do you know, my little dear, I am afraid, if you want to know, you must ask some of these vulgar birds about, for I have quite forgotten."

And the poor old Gairfowl began to cry tears of pure oil; and Tom was quite sorry for her; and for himself too, for he was at his wits' end whom to ask.

But by there came a flock of petrels, who are Mother Carey's own chickens; and Tom thought them much prettier than Lady Gairfowl, and so perhaps they were; for Mother Carey had had a great deal of fresh experience between the time that she invented the Gairfowl and the time that she invented them. They flitted along like a flock of black swallows, and hopped and skipped from wave to wave, lifting up their little feet behind them so daintily, and whistling to each other so tenderly, that Tom fell in love with them at once, and called them to know the way to Shiny Wall.

"Shiny Wall? Do you want Shiny Wall? Then come with us, and we will show you. We are Mother Carey's own chickens, and she sends us out over all the seas, to show the good birds the way home."

Tom was delighted, and swam off to them, after he had made his bow to the Gairfowl. But she would not return his bow: but held herself bolt upright, and wept tears of oil as she sang:

> " And so the poor stone was left all alone ;
> With a fal-lal-la-lady."

And now Tom was all agog to start for Shiny Wall; but the petrels said no. They must go first to Allfowlsness, and wait there for the great gathering of all the sea-birds, before they start for their summer breeding-places far away in the Northern Isles; and there they would be sure to find some birds which were going to Shiny Wall: but where Allfowlsness was, he must promise never to tell, lest men should go there and shoot the birds, and stuff them, and put them into stupid museums, instead of leaving them to play and

breed and work in Mother Carey's water-garden
where they ought to be.

So where Allfowlsness is nobody must
know; and all that is to be said about it is, that
Tom waited there many days.

And after a while the birds began to gather
at Allfowlsness, in thousands and tens of
thousands, blackening all the air; and they
paddled and washed and splashed and combed
and brushed themselves on the sand, till the
shore was white with feathers; and they
quacked and clucked and gabbled and chattered
and screamed and whooped as they talked over
matters with their friends, and settled where
they were to go and breed that summer, till
you might have heard them ten miles off; and
lucky it was for them that there was no one
to hear them but the old keeper, who lived all
alone upon the Ness, in a turf hut thatched
with heather and fringed round with great
stones slung across the roof by bent-ropes, lest

the winter gales should blow the hut right away. But he never minded the birds nor hurt them : only, when all the birds were going, he

toddled out, and took off his cap to them, and wished them a merry journey and a safe return ; and then gathered up all the feathers which they had left, and cleaned them to sell

down south, and make feather-beds for stuffy
people to lie on.

Then the petrels asked this bird and that
whether they would take Tom to Shiny Wall:
but one set was going to Sutherland, and one
to the Shetlands, and one to Norway, and one
to Spitzbergen, and one to Iceland, and one to
Greenland: but none would go to Shiny Wall.
So the good-natured petrels said that they
would show him part of the way themselves,
but they were only going as far as Jan Mayen's
Land; and after that he must shift for himself.

And then all the birds rose up, and streamed
away in long black lines, north, and north-east,
and north-west, across the bright blue summer
sky; and their cry was like ten thousand packs
of hounds, and ten thousand peals of bells.
Only the puffins stayed behind, and killed the
young rabbits, and laid their eggs in the rabbit-
burrows.

And, as Tom and the petrels went north-eastward, it began to blow right hard, till you could not see where the sky ended and the sea began. But Tom and the petrels never cared, for the gale was right abaft, and away they went over the crests of the billows, as merry as so many flying-fish.

And at last they saw an ugly sight—the black side of a great ship, water-logged in the trough of the sea. Her funnel and her masts were overboard, and swayed and surged under her lee; her decks were swept as clean as a barn floor, and there was no living soul on board.

The petrels flew up to her, and wailed round her; for they were very sorry indeed, and also they expected to find some salt pork; and Tom scrambled on board of her and looked round, frightened and sad.

And there, in a little cot, lashed tight under the bulwark, lay a baby fast asleep; the very same baby, Tom saw at once, which he had seen in the singing lady's arms.

He went up to it, and wanted to wake it; but behold, from under the cot out jumped a little black and tan terrier dog, and began barking and snapping at Tom, and would not let him touch the cot.

Tom knew the dog's teeth could not hurt him : but at least it could shove him away, and did ; and he and the dog fought and struggled, for he wanted to help the baby, and did not want to throw the poor dog overboard : but as they were struggling, there came a tall green sea, over the side of the ship, and swept them all into the waves.

" Oh, the baby, the baby ! " screamed Tom : but the next moment he did not scream at all; for he saw the cot settling down through the green water, with the baby, smiling in it, fast asleep; and he saw the fairies come up from below, and carry baby and cradle gently down in their soft arms; and then he knew it was all right, and that there would be a new water-baby in St. Brandan's Isle.

And the poor little dog?

Why, after he had kicked and coughed a little, he sneezed so hard, that he sneezed himself clean out of his skin, and turned into a water-dog, and jumped and danced round Tom, and ran over the crests of the waves, and snapped at the jelly-fish and the mackerel, and followed Tom the whole way to the Other-end-of-Nowhere.

Then they went on again, till they began to see the peak of Jan Mayen's Land, standing up like a white sugar-loaf, two miles above the clouds.

And there they fell in with a whole flock of molly-mocks, who were feeding on a dead whale.

"These are the fellows to show you the way," said Mother Carey's chickens; "we cannot help you farther north. We don't like to get among the ice-pack, for fear it should nip our toes: but the mollys dare fly anywhere."

So the petrels called to the mollys: but they were so busy and greedy, gobbling and pecking and spluttering and fighting over the blubber, that they did not take the least notice.

"Come, come," said the petrels, "you lazy greedy lubbers, this young gentleman is going

to Mother Carey, and if you don't attend on him, you won't earn your discharge from her, you know."

"Greedy we are," says a great fat old molly, "but lazy we ain't; and, as for lubbers, we're no more lubbers than you. Let's have a look at the lad."

And he flapped right into Tom's face, and stared at him in the most impudent way, and then asked him where he hailed from, and what land he sighted last.

And, when Tom told him, he seemed pleased, and said he was a good plucked one to have got so far.

" Come along, lads," he said to the rest, "and give this little chap a cast over the pack, for Mother Carey's sake. We've eaten blubber enough for to-day, and we'll e'en work out a bit of our time by helping the lad."

So the mollys took Tom up on their backs, and flew off with him, laughing and joking —and oh, how they did smell of train oil !

And now they came to the edge of the pack, and beyond it they could see Shiny Wall looming, through mist, and snow, and storm. But the pack rolled horribly upon the swell, and the ice giants fought and roared, and leapt upon each other's backs, and ground each other to powder, so that Tom was afraid to venture among them, lest he should be ground to powder too. And he was the more afraid, when he saw lying among the ice pack the wrecks of many a gallant ship; some with masts and yards all standing, some with the seamen frozen fast on board. Alas, alas, for them! They were all true English hearts.

But the good mollys took Tom and his dog up, and flew with them safe over the pack and the roaring ice giants, and set them down at the foot of Shiny Wall.

"And where is the gate?" asked Tom.

"There is no gate," said the mollys.

"No gate?" cried Tom, aghast.

"None; never a crack of one."

"What am I to do, then?"

"Dive under the floe, to be sure, if you have pluck."

"I've not come so far to turn now," said Tom; "so here goes for a header."

"A lucky voyage to you, lad," said the mollys; "we knew you were one of the right sort. So good-bye."

"Why don't you come too?" asked Tom.

But the mollys only wailed sadly, "We can't go yet, we can't go yet," and flew away over the pack.

So Tom dived under the great white gate which never was opened yet, and went on in black darkness, at the bottom of the sea, for seven days and seven nights. And yet he was not a bit frightened. Why should he be? He was a brave English lad, whose business is to go out and see all the world.

And at last he saw the light, and clear clear water overhead; and up he came a thousand fathoms, among clouds of sea-moths, which fluttered round his head. The dog snapped at them till his jaws were tired; but

THAT'S MOTHER CAREY, THERE SHE SITS MAKING OLD BEASTS INTO
NEW ALL THE YEAR ROUND

Tom hardly minded them at all, he was so eager to get to the top of the water, and see the pool where the good whales go.

And a very large pool it was, miles and miles across, though the air was so clear that the ice cliffs on the opposite side looked as if they were close at hand. All round it the ice cliffs rose, in walls and spires and battlements, and caves and bridges, and stories and galleries, in which the ice-fairies live, and drive away the storms and clouds, that Mother Carey's pool may lie calm from year's end to year's end. And the sun acted policeman, and walked round outside every day, peeping just over the top of the ice wall, to see that all went right; and now and then he played conjuring tricks, or had an exhibition of fireworks, to amuse the ice-fairies. For he would make himself into four or five suns at once, or paint the sky with rings and crosses and crescents of white fire, and stick himself in the middle of them, and

Q

wink at the fairies ; and I daresay they were very much amused ; for anything's fun in the country.

And there the good whales lay, the happy sleepy beasts, upon the still oily sea. They were all right whales, you must know, and finners, and razor-backs, and bottle-noses, and spotted sea-unicorns with long ivory horns. But the sperm whales are such raging, ramping, roaring, rumbustious fellows, that, if Mother Carey let them in, there would be no more peace in Peacepool. So she packs them away in a great pond by themselves at the South Pole, two hundred and sixty-three miles south-south-east of Mount Erebus, the great volcano in the ice ; and there they butt each other with their ugly noses, day and night from year's end to year's end.

But here there were only good quiet beasts, lying about, and blowing every now and then jets of white steam, or sculling round with their huge mouths open, for the sea-moths to swim down their throats. They were quite safe and happy there; and all they had to do was to wait quietly in Peacepool, till Mother Carey sent for them to make them out of old beasts into new.

Tom swam up to the nearest whale, and asked the way to Mother Carey.

"There she sits in the middle," said the whale.

Tom looked; but he could see nothing in the middle of the pool, but one peaked iceberg: and he said so.

"That's Mother Carey," said the whale, "as you will find when you get to her. There she sits making old beasts into new all the year round."

"How does she do that?"

"That's her concern, not mine," said the old whale; and yawned so wide (for he was very large) that there swam into his mouth

943 sea-moths, 13,846 jelly-fish no bigger than pins' heads, and forty-three little ice-crabs.

"I suppose," said Tom, "she cuts up a great whale like you into a whole shoal of porpoises?"

At which the old whale laughed so violently that he coughed up all the creatures; who swam away again very thankful at having escaped out of that terrible whalebone net of his, from which bourne no traveller returns; and Tom went on to the iceberg, wondering.

CHAPTER XV

WHEN he came near it, it took the form of the grandest old lady he had ever seen—a white marble lady, sitting on a white marble throne. And from the foot of the throne there swam away, out and out into the sea, millions of new-born creatures, of more shapes and colours than man ever dreamed. And they were Mother Carey's children, whom she makes out of the sea-water all day long.

He expected of course—like some grown people who ought to know better—to find her snipping, piecing, fitting, stitching, cobbling, basting, filing, planing, hammering, turning, polishing, moulding, measuring, chiselling,

clipping, and so forth, as men do when they
go to work to make anything.

But, instead of that, she sat quite still with

her chin upon her hand, looking down into
the sea with two great grand blue eyes, as blue
as the sea itself. Her hair was as white as
the snow—for she was very very old—in fact,

as old as anything which you are likely to come across.

And, when she saw Tom, she looked at him very kindly.

"What do you want, my little man? It is long since I have seen a water-baby here."

Tom told her his errand, and asked the way to the Other-end-of-Nowhere.

"You ought to know yourself, for you have been there already."

"Have I, ma'am? I'm sure I forget all about it."

"Then look at me."

And, as Tom looked into her great blue eyes, he recollected the way perfectly.

Now, was not that strange?

"Thank you, ma'am," said Tom. "Then I won't trouble your ladyship any more; I hear you are very busy."

"I am never more busy than I am now," she said, without stirring a finger.

"I heard, ma'am, that you were always making new beasts out of old."

"So people fancy. But I am not going to trouble myself to make things, my little dear. I sit here and make them make themselves."

"You are a clever fairy, indeed," thought Tom. And he was quite right.

"And now, my pretty little man," said Mother Carey, "you are sure you know the way to the Other-end-of-Nowhere?"

Tom thought; and behold, he had forgotten it utterly.

"That is because you took your eyes off me."

Tom looked at her again, and recollected; and then looked away, and forgot in an instant.

"But what am I to do, ma'am? For I can't keep looking at you when I am somewhere else."

"You must do without me, as most people have to do; and look at the dog instead; for he knows the way well enough, and will not forget it. Besides, you may meet some very queer-tempered people there, who will not let you pass without this passport of mine, which you must hang round your neck and take care of; and, of course, as the dog will always go behind you, you must go the whole way backward."

"Backward!" cried Tom. "Then I shall not be able to see my way."

"On the contrary, if you look forward, you will not see a step before you, and be certain to go wrong; but, if you look behind you, and watch carefully whatever you have passed, and especially keep your eye on the dog, who goes by instinct, and therefore can't go wrong, then you will know what is coming next, as plainly as if you saw it in a looking-glass."

Tom was very much astonished: but he

obeyed her, for he had learnt always to believe what the fairies told him.

He was very sorely tried; for though, by keeping the dog to heels (or rather to toes, for

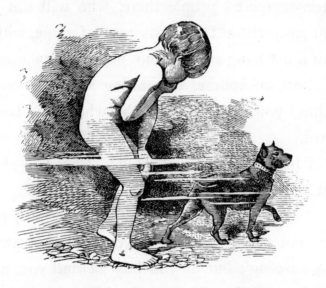

he had to walk backward), he could see pretty well which way the dog was hunting, yet it was much slower work to go backwards than to go forwards. But, what was more trying still, no sooner had he got out of Peacepool, than there came running to him all the conjurors, fortune-tellers, astrologers, prophesiers, as many as were in those parts, all bawling and screaming at him, "Look a-head, only look a-head; and we will show you what man never saw before, and right away to the end of the world!"

But I am proud to say that Tom was such a little dogged, hard English boy, that he never turned his head round once all the way from Peacepool to the Other-end-of-Nowhere: but kept his eye on the dog, and let him pick out the scent, hot or cold, straight or crooked, wet or dry, up hill or down dale; by which means he never made a single mistake, and saw all the wonderful things, which it is my duty to relate to you in the next chapter.

CHAPTER XVI

TOM'S JOURNEY TO THE OTHER-END-OF-NOWHERE, AND HIS ADVENTURES THEREIN

"Come to me, O ye children!
  For I hear you at your play;
And the questions that perplexed me
  Have vanished quite away.

"For what are all our contrivings
  And the wisdoms of our books,
When compared with your caresses,
  And the gladness of your looks?

"Ye open the Eastern windows,
  That look towards the sun,
Where thoughts are singing swallows,
  And the brooks of morning run.

" Ye are better than all the ballads
  That ever were sung or said;
For ye are living poems,
  And all the rest are dead."

                                              LONGFELLOW.

*   *   *   *

ERE begins the account of the nine-hundred-and-ninety-ninth part of the wonderful things which Tom saw on his journey to the Other-end-of-Nowhere.

Now, as soon as Tom had left Peace-pool, he came to the white lap of the great sea-mother, ten thousand fathoms deep; where she makes world-pap all day long, for the steam-giants to knead, and the fire-giants to bake, till it has risen and hardened into mountain-loaves and island-cakes.

And there Tom was very near being kneaded up in the world-pap, and turned into a fossil water-baby.

For, as he walked along in the silence of the sea-twilight, on the soft white ocean floor, he was aware of a hissing, and a roaring, and a thumping, and a pumping, as of all the steam-engines in the world at once. And, when he came near, the water grew boiling-hot ; not that that hurt him in the least : but it also grew foul ; and every moment he stumbled over dead shells, and fish, and sharks, and seals, and whales, which had been killed by the hot water.

And at last he came to the great sea-serpent himself, lying dead at the bottom ; and as he was too thick to scramble over, Tom had to walk round him three-quarters of a mile and more, which put him out of his path sadly ; and, when he had got round, he came to the place called Stop. And there he stopped, and just in time.

For he was on the edge of a vast hole in the bottom of the sea, up which was rushing

and roaring clear steam enough to work all the
engines in the world at once; so clear, indeed,
that it was quite light at moments; and Tom
could see almost up to the top of the water
above, and down below into the pit for nobody
knows how far.

But, as soon as he bent his head over the
edge, he got such a rap on the nose from
pebbles, that he jumped back again; for the
steam, as it rushed up, rasped away the sides
of the hole, and hurled it up into the sea in a
shower of mud and gravel and ashes; and then
it spread all around, and sank again, and covered
in the dead fish so fast, that before Tom had
stood there five minutes he was buried in silt
up to his ankles, and began to be afraid that
he should have been buried alive.

And perhaps he would have been, but that
while he was thinking, the whole piece of
ground on which he stood was torn off and
blown upwards, and away flew Tom a mile up

through the sea, wondering what was coming next.

At last he stopped—thump! and found himself tight in the legs of the most wonderful bogy which he had ever seen.

It had I don't know how many wings, as big as the sails of a windmill, and spread out in a ring like them; and with them it hovered over the steam which rushed up, as a ball hovers over the top of a fountain. And for every wing above it had a leg below, with a claw like a comb at the tip, and a nostril at the root; and in the middle it had no stomach and one eye; and as for its mouth, that was all on one side. Well, it was a very strange beast; but no stranger than some dozens which you may see.

"What do you want here," it cried quite peevishly, "getting in my way?" and it tried to drop Tom: but he held on tight to its claws, thinking himself safer where he was.

So Tom told him who he was, and what his errand was. And the thing winked its one eye and sneered :

"I am too old to be taken in in that way. You are come after gold—I know you are."

"Gold! What is gold?" And really Tom did not know ; but the suspicious old bogy would not believe him.

But after a while Tom began to understand a little. For, as the vapours came up out of the hole, the bogy smelt them with his nostrils, and combed them and sorted them with his combs ; and then, when they steamed up through them against his wings, they were changed into showers and streams of metal. From one wing fell gold-dust, and from another silver, and from another copper, and from another tin, and from another lead, and so on, and sank into the soft mud, into veins and cracks, and hardened there. Whereby it comes to pass that the rocks are full of metal.

R

But, all of a sudden, somebody shut off the steam below, and the hole was left empty in an instant: and then down rushed the water into the hole, in such a whirlpool that the bogy spun round and round as fast as a teetotum. But that was all in his day's work, like a fair fall with the hounds; so all he did was to say to Tom—

"Now is your time, youngster, to get down, if you are in earnest, which I don't believe."

"You'll soon see," said Tom; and away he went, as bold as Baron Munchausen, and shot down the rushing cataract like a salmon.

And, when he got to the bottom, he swam till he was washed on shore safe upon the Other-end-of-Nowhere.

And first he went through Waste-paper-land, where all the stupid books lie in heaps, up hill and down dale, like leaves in a winter wood; and there he saw people digging and grubbing among them, to make worse books out of bad ones; and a very good trade they drove thereby, especially among children.

He came to the place where every one knows his neighbour's business better than his own; and when he got into the middle of the town, they all set on him at once, to show him his way; or rather, to show him that he did not know his way; for as for asking him what way he wanted to go, no one ever thought of that.

But one pulled him hither, and another poked him thither, and a third cried—

"You mustn't go west, I tell you; it is destruction to go west."

"But I am not going west, as you may see," said Tom.

And another, "The east lies here, my dear; I assure you this is the east."

"But I don't want to go east," said Tom.

"Well, then, at all events, whichever way you are going, you are going wrong," cried they all with one voice—which was the only thing which they ever agreed about; and all pointed at once to all the thirty-and-two-points of the compass, till Tom thought all the sign-posts in England had got together, and fallen fighting.

And whether he would have ever escaped out of the town, it is hard to say, if the dog had not taken it into his head that they were going to pull his master in pieces, and tackled them so sharply about the legs, that he gave them some business of their own to think of at last; and while they were rubbing their bitten calves, Tom and the dog got safe away.

On the borders of that island he found Gotham, where the wise men live; the same who dragged the pond because the moon had fallen into it, and planted a hedge round the cuckoo, to keep spring all the year. And he found them bricking up the town gate, because

it was so wide that little folks could not get
through.   He could not help saying that in
his country, if the kitten could not get in at
the same hole as the cat, she might stay outside
and mew.

But he saw the end of such fellows, when
he came to the island of the Golden Asses,
where nothing but thistles grow.   For there
they were all turned into mokes with ears a
yard long, for meddling with matters which
they do not understand.

Then Tom came to a very famous island,
the Isle of Tomtoddies, all heads and no
bodies.

And when Tom came near it, he heard such
a grumbling and grunting and growling and
wailing and weeping and whining that he
thought people must be ringing little pigs, or
cropping puppies' ears, or drowning kittens :
but when he came nearer still, he began to
hear words among the noise ; which was the

Tomtoddies' song which they sing morning and evening, and all night too—

" I can't learn my lesson : the examiner's coming ! "

And that was the only song which they knew.

And when Tom got on shore the first thing he saw was a great pillar, on one side of which was inscribed, "Playthings not allowed here"; at which he was so shocked that he would not stay to see what was written on the other side. Then he looked round for the people of the island: but instead of men, women, and children, he found nothing but turnips and radishes, without a single green leaf among them, and half of them burst and decayed, with toad-stools growing out of them. Those which were left began crying to Tom, in half-a-dozen different languages at once, and all of them badly spoken, "I can't learn my lesson; do come and help me!"

"And what good on earth would it do you if I did?" quoth Tom.

Well, they didn't know that: all they knew was the examiner was coming.

Then Tom stumbled on the hugest and

softest turnip you ever saw, and it cried to him, "Can you tell me anything at all about anything you like?"

"About what?" says Tom.

"About anything you like; for as fast as I learn things I forget them again. So my mamma says that my intellect is not adapted for science, and says that I must go in for general information."

Tom told him that he did not know general information, nor any officers in the army; only he had a friend once that went for a drummer: but he could tell him a great many strange things which he had seen in his travels.

So he told him prettily enough, while the poor turnip listened very carefully; and the more he listened, the more he forgot, and the more water ran out of him.

Tom thought he was crying: but it was only his poor brains running away, from being worked so hard; and as Tom talked, the unhappy turnip streamed down all over with juice, and split and shrank till nothing was left of him but rind and water; whereat Tom ran away in a fright, for he thought he might be taken up for killing the turnip.

Tom was so puzzled and frightened with

all he saw, that he was longing to ask the
meaning of it ; and at last he stumbled over
a respectable old stick lying half covered with
earth.   But a very stout and worthy stick it
was.

"You see," said the stick, "there were as
pretty little children once as you could wish to
see, and might have been so still if they had
been only left to grow up like human beings,
and then handed over to me ; but their foolish
fathers and mothers, instead of letting them
pick flowers, and make dirt-pies, and get birds'
nests, and dance round the gooseberry bush, as
little children should, kept them always at
lessons, working, working, working, learning
week-day lessons all week-days, and Sunday
lessons all Sunday, and weekly examinations
every Saturday, and monthly examinations
every month, and yearly examinations every
year, everything seven times over, as if once
was not enough, and enough as good as a

feast—till their brains grew big, and their
bodies grew small, and they were all changed
into turnips, with little but water inside."

"Ah!" said Tom, "if dear Mrs. Doasyouwouldbedoneby knew of it she would send
them a lot of tops, and balls, and marbles,
and ninepins, and make them all as jolly as
sand-boys."

"It would be no use," said the stick.
"They can't play now, if they tried. Don't
you see how their legs have turned to roots
and grown into the ground, by never taking
any exercise, but sapping and moping always
in the same place? But here comes the
Examiner-of-all-Examiners. So you had better
get away, I warn you, or he will examine you
and your dog into the bargain, and set him to
examine all the other dogs, and you to examine
all the other water-babies. There is no escap-
ing out of his hands, for his nose is nine
thousand miles long, and can go down

chimneys, and through keyholes, upstairs, downstairs, in my lady's chamber, examining all little boys, and the little boys' tutors like-wise. But when he is thrashed—so Mrs. Be-donebyasyoudid has promised me—I shall have the thrashing of him : and if I don't lay it on with a will it's a pity."

Tom went off : but rather slowly and surlily ; for he was somewhat minded to face this same Examiner-of-all-Examiners, who came striding among the poor turnips, binding heavy burdens and grievous to be borne, and laying them on little children's shoulders.

But when he got near, he looked so big and burly and dictatorial, and shouted so loud to Tom, to come and be examined, that Tom ran for his life, and the dog too. And really it was time; for the poor turnips, in their hurry and fright, crammed themselves so fast to be ready for the Examiner, that they burst and popped by dozens all round him, and Tom thought he should be blown into the air, dog and all.

He went down to the shore and jumped into the sea, and swam on his way, singing :—

> " *Farewell Tomtoddies, all ; I thank my stars*
> *That nought I know save those three royal r's :*
> *Reading and riting sure, with rithmetick,*
> *Will help a lad of sense through thin and thick.*"

Whereby you may see that Tom was no poet.

And next he came to Oldwivesfabledom, where the folks were all heathens.

And there he found a little boy sitting in the middle of the road, and crying bitterly.

"What are you crying for?" said Tom.

" Because I am not as frightened as I could wish to be."

" Not frightened ? You are a queer little chap : but, if you want to be frightened, here goes—Boo ! "

" Ah," said the little boy, " that is very kind

of you; but I don't feel that it has made any impression."

Tom offered to upset him, punch him, stamp on him, fettle him over the·head with a brick, or anything else whatsoever which would give him the slightest comfort.

But he only thanked Tom very civilly, in fine long words which he had heard other folk use, and which, therefore, he thought were fit and proper to use himself; and cried on till his papa and mamma came, and sent off for the Powwow man immediately. And a very good-natured gentleman and lady they were, though they were heathens; and talked quite pleasantly to Tom about his travels, till the Powwow man arrived, with his thunderbox under his arm.

And a well-fed, ill-favoured gentleman he was. Tom was a little frightened at first; for he thought it was Grimes. But he soon saw his mistake: for Grimes always looked a man

in the face; and this fellow never did. And
when he spoke, it was fire and smoke; and
when he sneezed, it was squibs and crackers;
and when he cried, it was boiling pitch.

"Here we are again!" cried he, like the
clown in a pantomime. "So you can't feel
frightened, my little dear—eh? I'll do that
for you. I'll make an impression on you!
Yah! Boo! Whirroo! Hullabaloo!"

And he rattled, thumped, brandished his
thunderbox, yelled, shouted, raved, roared,
stamped, and danced; and then he touched a
spring in the thunderbox, and out popped
turnip-ghosts and magic-lanthorns and paste-
board bogies and spring-heeled Jacks, with
such a horrid din, clatter, clank, roll, rattle,
and roar, that the little boy turned up the
whites of his eyes, and fainted right away.

And at that his poor heathen papa and
mamma were delighted; and fell down upon
their knees before the Powwow man, and gave

him a palanquin with a pole of solid silver and curtains of cloth of gold; and carried him about in it on their own backs: but as soon as they had taken him up, the pole stuck to their shoulders, and they could not set him down any more, which was a pitiable sight to see. But you see, they had chosen to do a foolish thing just once too often; so, by the laws of Mrs. Bedonebyasyoudid, they had to go on doing it whether they chose or not.

Ah! don't you wish that some one would go and convert those poor heathens, and teach them not to frighten their little children into fits?

"Now, then," said the Powwow man to Tom, "wouldn't you like to be frightened, my little dear? For I can see plainly that you are a very wicked, naughty boy."

"You're another," quoth Tom, very sturdily. And when the man ran at him, and cried "Boo!" Tom ran at him in return, and cried

"Boo!" likewise, right in his face, and set the little dog upon him; and at his legs the dog went.

At which, if you will believe it, the fellow turned tail, thunderbox and all, and ran for his life, screaming, "Help! thieves! murder! fire! He is going to kill me! I am a ruined man! He will murder me; and break, burn, and destroy my precious and invaluable thunderbox; and then you will have no more thundershowers in the land. Help! help! help!"

At which the papa and mamma and all the people of Oldwivesfabledom flew at Tom, shouting, "Oh, the wicked, impudent, hard-hearted, graceless boy! Beat him, kick him, shoot him, drown him, hang him, burn him!" and so forth: but luckily they had nothing to shoot, hang, or burn him with, for the fairies had hid all the killing-tackle out of the way a little while before; so they could only pelt him with stones; and some of the stones went clean

through him, and came out the other side.
But he did not mind that a bit; for the holes
closed up again as fast as they were made,
because he was a water-baby. However, he
was very glad when he was safe out of the
country, for the noise there made him all but
deaf.

Then he came to a very quiet place, called
Leaveheavenalone. And there the sun was
drawing water out of the sea to make steam-
threads, and the wind was twisting them up
to make cloud-patterns, till they had worked
between them the loveliest lace, and hung it
up in their own Crystal Palace; while the good
old sea never grudged, for she knew they would
pay her back honestly. So the sun span, and
the wind wove, and all went well with the great
steam-loom.

CHAPTER XVII

TOM REACHES MR. GRIMES

AT last, after innumerable adventures, each more wonderful than the last, he saw before him a huge building.

Tom walked towards this great building, wondering what it was, and having a strange fancy that he might find Mr. Grimes inside it, till he saw running toward him, and shouting "Stop!" three or four people, who, when they came nearer, were nothing else than policemen's truncheons, running along without legs or arms.

Tom was not astonished. He was long past that. Neither was he frightened; for he had been doing no harm.

So he stopped; and, when the foremost

truncheon came up and asked his business, he
showed Mother Carey's pass ; and the truncheon
looked at it in the oddest fashion ; for he had
one eye in the middle of his upper end, so that

when he looked at anything, being quite stiff,
he had to slope himself, and poke himself, till
it was a wonder why he did not tumble over.

" All right—pass on," said he at last. And
then he added : " I had better go with you,

young man." And Tom had no objection, for such company was both respectable and safe; so the truncheon coiled its thong neatly round its handle, to prevent tripping itself up—for the thong had got loose in running—and marched on by Tom's side.

"Why have you no policeman to carry you?" asked Tom, after a while.

"Because we are not like those clumsy-made truncheons in the land-world, which cannot go without having a whole man to carry them about. We do our own work for ourselves; and do it very well."

"Then why have you a thong to your handle?" asked Tom.

"To hang ourselves up by, of course, when we are off duty."

Tom had got his answer, and had no more to say, till they came up to the great iron door of the prison. And there the truncheon knocked twice, with its own head.

A wicket in the door opened, and out
looked a tremendous old brass blunderbuss

charged up to the muzzle with slugs, who was
the porter; and Tom started back a little at
the sight of him.

"What case is this?" he asked in a deep voice, out of his broad bell mouth.

"If you please, sir, it is no case; only a young gentleman from her ladyship, who wants to see Grimes, the master-sweep."

"Grimes?" said the blunderbuss. And he pulled in his muzzle, perhaps to look over his prison-lists.

"Grimes is up chimney No. 345," he said from inside. "So the young gentleman had better go on to the roof."

Tom looked up at the enormous wall, which seemed at least ninety miles high, and wondered how he should ever get up: but, when he hinted that to the truncheon, it settled the matter in a moment. For it whisked round, and gave him such a shove behind as sent him up to the roof in no time, with his little dog under his arm.

And there he walked along the leads, till he met another truncheon, and told him his errand.

"Very good," it said. "Come along : but it will be of no use. He is the most unremorseful, hard-hearted, foul-mouthed fellow I have in charge ; and thinks about nothing but beer and pipes, which are not allowed here, of course."

So they walked along over the leads, and very sooty they were, and Tom thought the chimneys must want sweeping very much. But he was surprised to see that the soot did not stick to his feet, or dirty them in the least. Neither did the live coals, which were lying about in plenty, burn him, being a water-baby.

And at last they came to chimney No. 345. Out of the top of it, his head and shoulders just showing, stuck poor Mr. Grimes, so sooty, and bleared, and ugly, that Tom could hardly bear to look at him. And in his mouth was a pipe ; but it was not a-light ; though he was pulling at it with all his might.

"Attention, Mr. Grimes," said the

truncheon; "here is a gentleman come to see you."

But Mr. Grimes only said bad words; and kept grumbling, "My pipe won't draw. My pipe won't draw."

"Keep a civil tongue, and attend!" said the truncheon; and popped up just like Punch, hitting Grimes such a crack over the head with itself, that his brains rattled inside like a dried walnut in its shell. He tried to get his hands out, and rub the place: but he could not. for they were stuck fast in the chimney. Now he was forced to attend.

"Hey!" he said, "why, it's Tom! I suppose you have come here to laugh at me, you spiteful little atomy?"

Tom assured him he had not, but only wanted to help him.

"I don't want anything except beer, and that I can't get; and a light to this bothering pipe, and that I can't get either."

" I'll get you one," said Tom ; and he took up a live coal (there were plenty lying about) and put it to Grimes' pipe : but it went out instantly.

"It's no use," said the truncheon, leaning itself up against the chimney and looking on. "I tell you, it is no use. His heart is so cold that it freezes everything that comes near him. You will see that presently, plain enough."

"Oh, of course, it's my fault. Everything's always my fault," said Grimes. "Now don't go to hit me again " (for the truncheon started upright, and looked very wicked); "you know, if my arms were only free, you daren't hit me then."

The truncheon leant back against the chimney, and took no notice of the personal insult, like a well-trained policeman as it was.

"But can't I help you in any other way? Can't I help you to get out of this chimney?" said Tom.

" No," interposed the truncheon ; "he has

come to the place where everybody must help themselves; and he will find it out, I hope, before he has done with me."

"Oh, yes," said Grimes, "of course it's me. Did I ask to be brought here into the prison? Did I ask to be set to sweep your foul chimneys? Did I ask to have lighted straw put under me to make me go up? Did I ask to stick fast in the very first chimney of all, because it was so shamefully clogged up with soot? Did I ask to stay here—I don't know how long—a hundred years, I do believe, and never get my pipe, nor my beer, nor nothing fit for a beast, let alone a man?"

"No," answered a solemn voice behind. "No more did Tom, when you behaved to him in the very same way."

It was Mrs. Bedonebyasyoudid. And, when the truncheon saw her, it started bolt upright—Attention!—and made such a low bow. And Tom made his bow too.

"Oh, ma'am," he said, "don't think about me; that's all past and gone, and good times and bad times and all times pass over. But may not I help poor Mr. Grimes? Mayn't I try and get some of these bricks away, that he may move his arms?"

"You may try, of course," she said.

So Tom pulled and tugged at the bricks: but he could not move one. And then he tried to wipe Mr. Grimes' face: but the soot would not come off.

"Oh, dear!" he said. "I have come all this way, through all these terrible places, to help you, and now I am of no use at all."

"You had best leave me alone," said Grimes; "you are a good-natured forgiving little chap, and that's truth; but you'd best be off. The hail's coming on soon, and it will beat the eyes out of your little head."

"What hail?"

"Why, hail that falls every evening here;

and, till it comes close to me, it's like so much warm rain : but then it turns to hail over my head, and knocks me about like small shot."

"That hail will never come any more," said the strange lady. "I have told you before what it was. It was your mother's tears, those which she shed when she prayed for you by her bedside ; but your cold heart froze it into hail. But she is gone to heaven now, and will weep no more for her graceless son."

Then Grimes was silent awhile ; and then he looked very sad.

"So my old mother's gone, and I never there to speak to her! Ah! a good woman she was, and might have been a happy one, in her little school there in Vendale, if it hadn't been for me and my bad ways."

"Did she keep the school in Vendale?" asked Tom. And then he told Grimes all the story of his going to her house, and how she could not abide the sight of a chimney-sweep, and then how kind she was, and how he turned into a water-baby.

"Ah!" said Grimes, "good reason she had to hate the sight of a chimney-sweep. I ran away from her and took up with the sweeps, and never let her know where I was, nor sent her a penny to help her, and now it's too late —too late!" said Mr. Grimes.

And he began crying and blubbering like a great baby, till his pipe dropped out of his mouth, and broke all to bits.

"Oh, dear, if I was but a little chap in Vendale again, to see the clear beck, and the apple-orchard, and the yew-hedge, how different I would go on! But it's too late now. So you go along, you kind little chap, and don't stand to look at a man crying, that's old enough to be your father, and never feared the face of man, nor of worse neither. But I'm beat now, and beat I must be. I've made my bed, and I must lie on it. Foul I would be, and foul I am, as an Irishwoman said to me once; and little I heeded it. It's all my own fault: but it's too late." And he cried so bitterly that Tom began crying too.

"Never too late," said the fairy, in such a strange soft new voice that Tom looked up at her; and she was so beautiful for the moment, that Tom half fancied she was her sister.

No more was it too late. For, as poor Grimes cried and blubbered on, his own tears did what his mother's could not do, and Tom's could not do, and nobody's on earth could do for him; for they washed the soot off his face and off his clothes; and then they washed the mortar away from between the bricks; and the chimney crumbled down; and Grimes began to get out of it.

Up jumped the truncheon, and was going to hit him on the crown a tremendous thump, and drive him down again like a cork into a bottle. But the strange lady put it aside.

"Will you obey me if I give you a chance?"

"As you please, ma'am. You're stronger than me—that I know too well, and wiser than me, I know too well also. And, as for being my own master, I've fared ill enough with that as yet. So whatever your ladyship pleases to order me ; for I'm beat, and that's the truth."

"Be it so then—you may come out. But remember, disobey me again, and into a worse place still you go."

"I beg pardon, ma'am, but I never disobeyed you that I know of. I never had the honour of setting eyes upon you till I came to these ugly quarters."

"Never saw me? Who said to you, Those that will be foul, foul they will be?"

Grimed looked up ; and Tom looked up too ; for the voice was that of the Irishwoman who met them the day that they went out together to Harthover. "I gave you your

I HAVE BEEN SITTING HERE WAITING FOR YOU MANY A HUNDRED
YEARS

warning then: but you gave it yourself a thousand times before and since. Every bad word that you said—every cruel and mean thing that you did—every time that you got tipsy—every day that you went dirty—you were disobeying me, whether you knew it or not."

" If I'd only known, ma'am——"

" You knew well enough that you were disobeying something, though you did not know it was me. But come out and take your chance. Perhaps it may be your last."

So Grimes stepped out of the chimney, and really, if it had not been for the scars on his face, he looked as clean and respectable as a master-sweep need look.

" Take him away," said she to the truncheon, " and give him his ticket-of-leave."

" And what is he to do, ma'am ? "

" Get him to sweep out the crater of Etna ; he will find some very steady men working out

T

their time there, who will teach him his business : but mind, if that crater gets choked again, and there is an earthquake in consequence, bring them all to me, and I shall investigate the case very severely."

So the truncheon marched off Mr. Grimes, looking as meek as a drowned worm.

And for aught I know, or do not know, he is sweeping the crater of Etna to this very day.

"And now," said the fairy to Tom, "your work here is done. You may as well go back again."

"I should be glad enough to go," said Tom, "but how am I to get up that great hole again, now the steam has stopped blowing?"

"I will take you up the backstairs : but I must bandage your eyes first; for I never allow anybody to see those backstairs of mine."

"I am sure I shall not tell anybody about them, ma'am, if you bid me not."

"Aha! So you think, my little man. But you would soon forget your promise if you got back into the land-world. So come—now I must bandage your eyes." So she tied the bandage on his eyes with one hand, and with the other she took it off.

"Now," she said, "you are safe up the stairs." Tom opened his eyes very wide, and his mouth too; for he had not, as he thought, moved a single step. But, when he looked round him, there could be no doubt that he was safe up the backstairs, whatsoever they may be.

The first thing which Tom saw was the black cedars, high and sharp against the rosy dawn; and St. Brandan's Isle reflected double in the still broad silver sea. The wind sang softly in the cedars, and the water sang among the caves: the sea-birds sang as they streamed out into the ocean, and the land-birds as they built among the boughs; and the air was full of song; but among all the songs one came across the water more sweet and clear than all; for it was the song of a young girl's voice.

And what was the song which she sang? Ah, my little man, I am too old to sing that song, and you too young to understand it. But have patience, and keep your eye single, and your hands clean, and you will learn some day to sing it yourself, without needing any man to teach you.

And as Tom neared the island, there sat upon a rock the most graceful creature that ever was seen, looking down, with her chin upon her hand, and paddling with her feet in the water. And when they came to her she looked up, and behold it was Ellie.

"Oh, Miss Ellie," said he, "how you are grown!"

"Oh, Tom," said she, "how you are grown too!"

And no wonder; they were both quite

grown up—he into a tall man, and she into a beautiful woman.

"Perhaps, I may be grown," she said. "I have had time enough; for I have been sitting here waiting for you many a hundred years, till I thought you were never coming."

"Many a hundred years?" thought Tom; but he had seen so much in his travels that he had quite given up being astonished; and, indeed, he could think of nothing but Ellie. So he stood and looked at Ellie, and Ellie looked at him; and they liked it so much that they neither spoke nor stirred.

At last they heard the fairy say: "Attention, children. Are you never going to look at me again?"

"We have been looking at you all this while," they said. And so they thought they had been.

"Then look at me once more," said she.

They looked—and both of them cried out at once, "Oh, who are you, after all?"

"You are our dear Mrs. Doasyouwouldbedoneby."

"No, you are good Mrs. Bedonebyasyoudid; but you are grown quite beautiful now!"

"To you," said the fairy. "But look again."

"You are Mother Carey," said Tom, in a very low, solemn voice; for he had found out something which made him very happy, and yet frightened him more than all that he had ever seen.

"But you are grown quite young again."

"To you," said the fairy. "Look again."

"You are the Irishwoman who met me the day I went to Harthover!"

And when they looked she was neither of them, and yet all of them at once.

"My name is written in my eyes, if you have eyes to see it there."

And they looked into her great, deep, soft eyes, and they changed again and again into every hue, as the light changes in a diamond.

" Now read my name," said she, at last.

And her eyes flashed, for one moment, clear, white, blazing light: but the children could not read her name; for they were dazzled, and hid their faces in their hands.

" Not yet, young things, not yet," said she, smiling; and then she turned to Ellie.

" You may take him home with you now on Sundays, Ellie. He has won his spurs in the great battle, and become fit to go with you and be a man; because he has done the thing he did not like."

So Tom went home with Ellie on Sundays, and sometimes on week-days, too; and he is now a great man of science, and can plan rail-roads, and steam-engines, and electric tele-graphs, and rifled guns, and so forth; and knows everything about everything. And all this from what he learnt when he was a water-baby, underneath the sea.

" And of course Tom married Ellie ? "

" And Tom's dog ? "

Oh, you may see him any clear night in July ; for the old dog-star was so worn out by the last three hot summers that there have been no dog-days since ; so that they had to take him down and put Tom's dog up in his place. And that is the end of my story.